DR S...
W...

BY
MARGARET BARKER

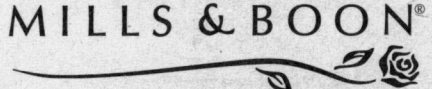

DID YOU PURCHASE THIS BOOK WITHOUT A COVER?
If you did, you should be aware it is **stolen property** as it was reported *unsold and destroyed* by a retailer. Neither the author nor the publisher has received any payment for this book.

All the characters in this book have no existence outside the imagination of the author, and have no relation whatsoever to anyone bearing the same name or names. They are not even distantly inspired by any individual known or unknown to the author, and all the incidents are pure invention.

All Rights Reserved including the right of reproduction in whole or in part in any form. This edition is published by arrangement with Harlequin Enterprises II B.V. The text of this publication or any part thereof may not be reproduced or transmitted in any form or by any means, electronic or mechanical, including photocopying, recording, storage in an information retrieval system, or otherwise, without the written permission of the publisher.

This book is sold subject to the condition that it shall not, by way of trade or otherwise, be lent, resold, hired out or otherwise circulated without the prior consent of the publisher in any form of binding or cover other than that in which it is published and without a similar condition including this condition being imposed on the subsequent purchaser.

MILLS & BOON and MILLS & BOON with the Rose Device are registered trademarks of the publisher.

*First published in Great Britain 2003
Harlequin Mills & Boon Limited,
Eton House, 18-24 Paradise Road, Richmond, Surrey TW9 1SR*

© Margaret Barker 2003

ISBN 0 263 83457 3

*Set in Times Roman 10½ on 12 pt.
03-0703-46715*

*Printed and bound in Spain
by Litografía Rosés, S.A., Barcelona*

CHAPTER ONE

AS FRANCESCA drew nearer to the shore the sea felt warmer. Although it was August, out there in the deep, deep water of the bay she'd felt decidedly chilly even though she'd struck out at a punishing pace. And when she'd opened her eyes under water to look at the shoals of inquisitive fish swimming near to her she'd felt something akin to vertigo as she'd stared down towards the seemingly fathomless bed of the sea in the middle of the bay.

For a few moments she rested on the surface of the water, imagining as she drifted along, totally relaxed, that she was floating on an airbed or else she was simply a piece of flotsam tossed into the water by a passing boat. Mmm, this was bliss! She raised her eyes to look at the hills on either side of the bay, marvelling at how steeply the hillsides swooped down into the water where they continued the same sheer drop towards the dark mysterious depths of the sea.

Emerging from the shallows, shaking herself to remove the droplets of water, the morning sun warmed her salty skin with its soothing rays as she turned her face upwards to look at the cloudless blue sky.

Oh, it was so good to be back on Ceres! The stones by the jetty were already warm to the touch of her bare feet as she picked up her towel and wrapped it around her bare white shoulders. This was what she'd missed for the past year in London. Sun, sea, relaxation and family. Looking up at the beautiful house that her father had bought on his retirement, Francesca wondered why she hadn't made time to come out here more often.

She'd felt like escaping here last summer when Jason had walked out on her. What had it been that had held her back? Her hospital career? Or had it been simply her wretched pride? As the eldest daughter, she'd never liked to admit that she couldn't handle her own life.

'Francesca! How was the swim?'

Shielding her eyes from the sun, she looked up at the ancient crenellated terrace at the front of the house and thought how incredibly young her mother looked, for a woman in her mid-fifties, as she leaned over the terrace wall. The long blonde hair which was usually wound up in a sophisticated chignon at the back of her head was still loose around her attractive, high-cheekboned face.

'Fantastic! I'd forgotten what a good idea it was to start the day with a swim.'

Francesca had got used to people saying she and her mother looked like sisters. They had the same bone structure, the same colouring.

'I'll come and give you a hand, Mum. What time is everybody arriving for lunch?'

Pam Metcalfe shrugged her slender shoulders and laughed. 'Midday GMT. That's Greek maybe time. We've got to have an early lunch because Michaelis and Sara have to go to Rhodes this afternoon to catch their flight to London. Demetrius and Chloe should be here soon.'

Pam paused to extricate a weed that had embedded itself in a crack in the ancient stonework.

'It's good to have you back, Francesca. How long are you planning to stay this time?'

Francesca was giving the question some thought as she ran up the stone steps that led to the terrace. She sank down on a wooden seat near her mother, rubbing herself vigorously with the towel.

'Francesca, how long did you say…?'

Francesca took a deep breath. 'Mum, did you know that Michaelis, has asked me to join the staff at the hospital?'

Pam's eyes widened. 'No, I didn't. But that would be wonderful…except I know you've been looking forward to having a holiday and travelling around for a few weeks. What have you decided?'

Final decision time. No more procrastination. Francesca looked out across the bay towards the hill above the shingly beach on the opposite shore as she gathered her thoughts.

On this side of the bay, a donkey, laden with a basket of oil and candles destined for one of the little chapels high in the hills was trotting up the path beside the house. A man on a second donkey turned to wave at Francesca.

Francesca waved back. Such friendly people! She remembered this man from holidays out here when she'd been much younger. They'd rented this house as a summer home in those days and, as a child, she'd been fascinated as she watched the donkeys trekking over the hills. How could anyone not want to live out here?

She turned to look at her mother who was still waiting for her answer. 'Before I arrived a couple of days ago, I'd decided not to change my plans about travelling for three months. Michaelis wrote to me about a month ago, explaining that as medical director at Ceres hospital he'd got a problem with staffing during the peak tourist season. He needed at least one more doctor to complete his medical team. He explained that as I was coming out for the wedding I could give him an answer when he saw me.'

'I think you'd enjoy working at the hospital, Francesca,' Pam said eagerly. 'Your sisters are very happy there.'

Francesca stretched out her toes towards the warming rays of the sun. 'Are you sure their happiness hasn't something to do with meeting their new husbands at the hospital?'

Pam smiled. 'I'm sure that has something to do with it. But it's an excellent hospital and the staff are so friendly.'

'When I arrived here from London, the day before their double wedding, I felt so tired I couldn't imagine starting a new job until I'd had a holiday. But working out here on Ceres isn't going to be like London, is it? I mean, I'll have times when I'm off duty and I can swim and walk over the hills just like I used to.'

'You sound as if you've made your mind up.'

Francesca nodded. 'I have. Out there in the deep water, watching the fish swimming beneath me, I knew I had to take this opportunity. I can go travelling later in the year when the need for extra doctors at the hospital isn't so acute.'

'We'll love having you home again. How long is it before you have to go back to London?'

Francesca took a deep breath. 'I've resigned, Mum. I've given myself three months to decide what I want to do next.'

Pam leaned forward in her chair. 'And Jason? Where does he figure in all of this?'

'He doesn't. That was over a long time ago.'

Francesca stood up, anxious to end what might be a lengthy discussion. She didn't want to think about Jason any more. She felt soothed by her morning swim and it would be a pity to spoil the atmosphere. She would get around to explaining the awful details of her disastrous relationship, but not now.

'I'm going for my shower. It looks as if people are arriving.'

As she spoke, Francesca pointed across the bay to the road that hugged the coast on the other side. There was a car coming along the road.

'I think that's Daddy returning from shopping in Ceres town,' Pam said. 'He took Rachel and Samantha with him.'

'I know. I was just going to go and see if they wanted to come swimming with me when I heard them running out to the car.'

Pam smiled. 'They would have enjoyed that. The twins adore you. They were so excited when they heard you were coming over for the wedding. Just wait till I tell them their aunt is going to be living here for a while!'

'I'm looking forward to seeing more of them.'

As she ran up the stairs to her bedroom, Francesca was thinking about her little nieces. Eight years old now. She remembered the day they were born so vividly.

A pang of anxiety ran through her. She'd thought she could handle being without children of her own but it didn't get any easier. Still, she could compensate by being a doting aunt. And her work in paediatrics had always been very satisfying.

The words of that old song came into her head again

and she sang softly as she turned on the water in the shower.

'Other people's children, that's my lot...'

Francesca showered quickly before pulling on a towelling robe to wear while she dried her hair. Stepping out onto the small balcony that led out from her bedroom, she saw that more cars were arriving now. Her sisters, Chloe and Sara, looking as radiant as only brides could on the day after their wedding, climbed out of a four-wheel-drive vehicle that had pulled up in front of the house. Demetrius and Michaelis, their tall, dark, handsome husbands, were helping them to jump down, holding them closely as they reached the ground.

Francesca looked away. She was so happy for her younger sisters, so glad that they'd found the men of their dreams. It was like a fairy-tale ending for both of them. Or was it a fairy-tale beginning? Either way, Chloe and Sara looked as if life was wonderful.

Back in her room, as Francesca searched for her hairdryer she could hear loud shouts of excitement from the twins as they greeted their parents, Chloe and Demetrius. It was fantastic that the four of them were a real family at last after all the years of being apart.

Plugging in the hairdryer, Francesca began to think about the beautiful wedding they'd celebrated yesterday. Chloe and Demetrius, Sara and Michaelis. Both couples so in love... She sighed as she ran her fingers through her hair and began teasing it into shape. If she'd said yes to Jason she would have been married a whole year by now.

And think what a disaster that would have been!

She ran a brush over her still damp hair. It would dry quickly in the sun out there on the terrace. She didn't want to spend any more time away from the family. Pulling on cotton trousers and a white cotton shirt, she ran down the back stairs to the kitchen.

Chloe and Sara were already helping their mother and Maria, their invaluable domestic help, preparing the vegetables and salads. Samantha and Rachel were sitting at the kitchen table, proudly rolling out pastry to make spinach pies.

'Look at my beautiful spanakopita, Francesca!' Rachel waved a flour-covered little arm towards her aunt. 'We made the pastry ourselves. It's not from a packet, is it, Maria?

Maria smiled happily at the little girls. 'You are very good cooks. When you finish this spanakopita, you can make tiropita for me.'

'Cheese pies!' Samantha said, reaching across to add more flour to the already dusty table. *'Horaya!'*

Francesca smiled at Chloe. 'The girls have really taken to the Greek way of life.

'They love going to school in the upper town. We're all going to live in Demetrius's house now and they're thrilled because it's near the school and lots of their friends live up there.'

Francesca looked at the joyful, serene expression on her newly married sister's face.

'You're going to be very happy with Demetrius.'

Chloe reached forwards and took hold of Francesca's hand. 'I never dreamed I could be so happy.'

'You both looked so radiant yesterday,' Francesca said, putting her arm around Sara's shoulders so that the three sisters were standing close together.

'It was the most wonderful day of my life,' Sara breathed.

Pam was looking admiringly at her daughters. 'It's good to see the three of you all together again—if only for a short while. Let's go upstairs and be sociable—that is, if Maria doesn't need us any more?'

'Thank you for helping,' Maria said. 'Now, please, go away and enjoy yourselves.'

'We haven't finished the spanakopita and the tiropita, Maria,' Rachel said.

Maria smiled fondly at the children. 'You must both stay and help me, of course.'

Maria had been the domestic help in this house for the past twenty years, even before the Metcalfe family had bought it. Pam and her daughters had always offered help when there'd been a big crowd coming for a meal, although there were times when Maria simply wanted to get on by herself. But she was always happy to have the children in the kitchen.

Stepping out onto the terrace with her sisters, Francesca was beginning to get nervous about her decision to join the staff of the hospital. Michaelis hadn't put any pressure on her. In fact, he'd only mentioned it once in his rather formal letter. Looking at Sara's husband now, deep in conversation with Demetrius, his medical colleague and new brother-in-law, and Anthony, her father, Francesca began to have second thoughts.

Would she feel like an outsider as a temporary doctor at the hospital? The last year had been traumatic and she really needed a rest from working. She'd saved enough money to travel for three months so there was no need to work. What if everything changed when she became one of the staff? It was one thing to have Michaelis and Demetrius as her brothers-in-law but—

'Francesca! I didn't see you come out here.' Michaelis stood up and walked across the terrace. He lowered his voice. 'So, have you given any thought to what I asked in my letter?'

Francesca took a deep breath. 'I'd like to join the staff for the rest of the busy tourist season, as you suggested. Until November.'

'You would?' Michaelis smiled. 'But that's excellent. Come over and meet another of our colleagues. This is Andonis, who used to specialise in orthopaedics but now has to deal with whatever kind of patients turn up at the hospital. Andonis, let me introduce you to my sister-in-law Francesca, who used to specialise in paediatrics in London but has just agreed to be a doctor in whichever department she will be needed.'

The genial Dr Andonis smiled as he stretched out his hand. 'Looking at the puzzled expression on your face, Francesca, I gather you didn't know you would have to be exceptionally versatile to survive in Ceres hospital.'

Francesca smiled. 'Well, it did come as something of a surprise after working in the paediatric unit of a large London hospital.'

She turned to look at Michaelis. 'What exactly will I…?'

'Excuse me, Francesca, there is another colleague arriving who I want you to meet.'

Michaelis hurried across the terrace. 'Sotiris, come and join us over here. This is Francesca, who hasn't worked with us before. That means that, as you're both newcomers, the two of you will have a lot in common.'

The man was very tall, with rugged, classic Mediterranean features, not handsome exactly, more striking than handsome, the sort of man she would like to get to know. A man who looked slightly uneasy at this gathering where everybody was either related or had worked with each other.

'Hello, Francesca.' Sotiris held out his hand to grasp hers. 'You're a raw recruit as well, I gather.'

'Looks like it.'

He had lovely grey eyes. She hadn't seen a man with grey eyes in Greece before. His hair was black, dark, smooth, long for a doctor. How old was he? Late thirties perhaps. Lines around the eyes. A hint of grey behind the ears. Hey, steady on! She realised she was really studying this man, something she hadn't done for a long time. Well, he looked interesting enough to spend some time with. Not boring, definitely not boring.

'I was just about to explain to Francesca that, even though she was a paediatric registrar in London, she will be expected to work wherever she is required at the hospital,' Michaelis said.

'We've found it's the easiest way of making full use of our staff in a relatively small hospital,' Andonis said. 'You'll soon get used to it. Obviously, if there's a patient who requires the specialist skills which one of our doctors has, we try to ensure that particular doctor is called in to work on the case.'

'Sotiris is a consultant surgeon in Athens,' Michaelis said. 'He's helping me out for three months by taking over as medical director while I'm away.'

Sotiris smiled. 'And Michaelis is helping me out by letting me spend some time on my favourite island.'

'You've obviously spent some time here,' Francesca said.

'I was born here.'

He had a fascinatingly low voice. Deeply reverberating, sort of *basso profundo*. He would look so good on stage in a Greek drama! He had that sort of impressive aura about him.

'You'll find the Ceres hospital something of a change from the large hospital where you work in Athens,' Francesca's father, Anthony, said, pausing long enough amongst the group to pour more wine into their glasses.

'I worked at Ceres hospital soon after I qualified,' Sotiris said quietly. 'It was much smaller in those days and wasn't so well equipped as it is now. But I wanted to pursue a surgical career. That was why I had to go to Athens. Sometimes I wish…'

Everyone had gone quiet. Sotiris stopped speaking and took a sip from the glass he was holding.

'Yes?' Anthony said, putting down the empty bottle on a nearby table. 'Were you going to say, you wished you'd stayed here?'

'I was indeed.'

Anthony nodded. 'I know the feeling. The life of a consultant surgeon is very rewarding but there is nothing to beat living on a beautiful island like this.'

Demetrius, having been called away to admire the cooking skills of his daughters, now rejoined the group with the twins holding tightly to his hands.

'Anthony was a consultant surgeon before his retirement, Sotiris,' Demetrius said.

'I know,' Sotiris said quietly. He turned to look at Anthony. 'I once came to one of your seminars in London, sir. Do you still give lectures?'

'Occasionally I dig out one of my suits and go over to Rhodes to talk to a class of medical students. I don't stay over there very long. I'm supposed to be retired now and this is where I'm happiest, with my family.'

'I was sorry to miss the wedding yesterday,' Sotiris

said. 'A double wedding is very rare. You must be sad to lose two of your daughters.'

Anthony smiled. 'I haven't lost Sara and Chloe. I've gained Demetrius and Michaelis. And my eldest daughter, Francesca, has finally decided to join us here after many years. We could never persuade her to leave her work in London before. Francesca is very ambitious—and successful. One of the youngest registrars in the hospital,' Anthony added, unable to disguise the pride in his voice.

'I've simply been too busy to get out here, Daddy,' Francesca said quickly.

Anthony put an arm round her shoulder. 'I know, darling. I was exactly like you for most of my professional life. You're a chip off the old block.'

'But it's different for a man, isn't it?' Sotiris said. 'A man feels it's his duty to be ambitious, whereas…'

He broke off, temporarily overawed by the fact that Francesca was taking an abnormally keen interest in what he had to say.

'Whereas what?' Francesca prompted quietly. 'Are you implying that a woman should have a different outlook on her career, simply because she's a woman?'

Sotiris hesitated. His initial appraisal of Francesca had been on a superficial level. She was a very beautiful woman. But she was already challenging his outlook on life. The outlook he'd been forced to adopt in the light of the trauma he'd suffered.

Sotiris cleared his throat. 'In my experience, it's much harder for a woman to have a successful career than it is for a man.'

'You're absolutely right,' Chloe said, joining the group as she handed round a bowl of olives. 'Juggling work and family life is never easy. As a full-time nursing Sister, I should know.'

Francesca swallowed hard. 'But there are some women who choose to have a career instead of a family.'

She raised her eyes to look at the other newcomer to the hospital. Sotiris was looking at her with a pained expression. This often happened when she propounded the myth that she was a dedicated career-woman and having a family wasn't an option for her.

Well, having a family wasn't an option, was it? But not in the way everybody thought. She never went on to elaborate further. Not until she became too involved in a relationship with someone and it was too late to explain how she really felt.

Jason had never understood her heartache.

Sotiris was looking down at her with a concerned expression. 'Do you really approve of the fact that some women ignore their biological destiny?'

Francesca gave a deliberately facetious laugh so as to lighten the atmosphere. She couldn't bear it when people became emotionally involved with the subject she liked to avoid.

'What a pompous expression! Biological destiny?'

'Forgive me if my English is a little archaic, Francesca,' Sotiris said. 'Let me put it another way. I believe that all women are biologically programmed to have children and so…'

'So do I,' Francesca said quietly. 'But…'

She broke off. If she was truthful, she would say that not all women were lucky enough to be able to fulfill their biological destiny. But that would open up an even more embarassing discussion and she would have to choose to opt out.

She realised Sotiris was waiting for her to continue. He didn't deserve to be treated like this. Biological destiny. That was a lovely phrase he'd used just now and she'd done nothing except try to ridicule him. His expression was understandably hostile now, which was a pity because she would have liked to have started off on a good footing with him as they were going to be medical colleagues.

Sotiris leaned forward towards her. 'But...? What was it you were going to say?'

Francesca pushed her long blonde hair back behind her ears. She would have to improvise so as to give some sort of coherent answer. 'I was going to say—'

'Francesca! Try one of my spanokopita,' called a childish voice.

Francesca leaned down and hugged Samantha, almost upsetting the large plate of spinach pies her niece was carrying. Saved in the nick of time!

'Thank you, Samantha. Would you like one, Sotiris?' Francesca smiled. 'A peace offering?'

Sotiris gave Francesca a wry grin as he took one of the tiny triangular packets of puff pastry and spinach.

'I'm glad to see that even dedicated career-women have a sense of humour.'

He swallowed the delicious spanakopita. 'Mmm, delicious. Thank you, Samantha,' he said as he looked down at the pretty little dark-haired girl. Her identical twin was trying to elbow her out of the way by pushing another plate towards him.

'Take one of my tiropita. I'm Rachel.'

'Thank you, Rachel,' Sotiris said. 'Did you make these yourself?'

'Of course,' Rachel said, scampering away across the terrace, scattering a couple of small pies on the cobblestones in her haste to show the pies to her grandmother.

Samantha followed more slowly, holding her plate with both hands. She paused to put her plate on a table so that she could bend down to pick up the pies that Rachel had dropped. Carefully, she dusted them off before placing them at the edge of her own plate.

Francesca smiled fondly as she watched her nieces. She was completely unaware that Sotiris was still looking at her. And she was also oblivious to the fact that he was trying to work out what made her tick.

For a few moments, Sotiris averted his eyes from the attractive woman in front of him. He'd only known her a few minutes and yet he felt as if he'd known her for years. That was because she was so obviously the career-woman type he now avoided like the plague. Once bitten, twice shy!

It was such a pity, because at the moment of introduction he'd been drawn to her beautiful smile, her obvious *joie de vivre*. He would have enjoyed working with her, even…well, even getting to know her a bit more. But under the circumstances he couldn't possibly allow himself to get to know her better. His life would become far too complicated if he did. Even more complicated than it was now!

'Lunch is ready,' Pam announced.

In spite of his aversion to the type of woman that Francesca personified, Sotiris couldn't help feeling glad when he found himself seated next to her at the large round table in the family dining room. She had a vivacious personality, she kept the conversation around her flowing easily and, obviously, everybody in her family adored her. Including her little nieces, who'd wanted to sit either side of her. Only their grandmother, who'd organised where everyone should sit, had been able to persuade them that she needed them to sit beside her so that they could give her some help.

Sotiris had seen how disappointed the little girls were not to be next to their aunt. Francesca seemed a natural with children—she was a paediatric registrar, for heaven's sake! So why had she chosen to deny herself the joys of motherhood?

As he put some taramasalata on the crusty homemade bread rolls, he glanced sideways at Francesca who was deep in animated conversation with Michaelis, seated across the table. He liked the way her whole face lit up when she spoke to one of the family members. There was no doubt they were a close-knit family. So why, when there was all this family love around, did Francesca choose to be the odd one out?

'So when can we expect you and Sara to return from your honeymoon travels, Michaelis?' Francesca was asking.

Michaelis smiled. 'We should be back by the end of November. We fly to London this evening for a couple of nights, after which we go to Singapore, Thailand, Hong Kong and finally to Australia.'

'I hope you won't get too tired with all this travelling,' Pam said.

Sara smiled. 'I don't think so, Mum. I've always wanted to do more travelling. We plan to be in Australia by October and then we're actually signed up to work in a hospital in Sydney for a few weeks. Michaelis arranged it with a friend of his from medical school who's a consultant there. We thought it would be a good experience for us.'

'And we'll also need to earn some money by then,' Michaelis said wryly. 'We've got our air tickets and enough for expenses until October. After our London honeymoon we won't be living in five-star luxury but it's going to be the trip of a lifetime.'

Sara reached across and squeezed her husband's hand. 'It's going to be fantastic, darling.'

'I would have liked to take Chloe and the girls on honeymoon but Chloe insisted she wanted to stay at home,' Demetrius said.

Chloe smiled fondly at her new husband. 'I want to enjoy living in my new home with you and the girls. They've got to go to school and—'

'I told you the girls could stay with me,' Pam said quickly. 'But I know how you love just being a family up there in that lovely house. Anyway, you can go off on a honeymoon at Christmas if you want, Chloe.'

'Thanks, Mum, but I'd rather stay on Ceres for Christmas,' Chloe said.

Watching her sister now, Francesca could see how happy she was to remain behind. With her wonderful husband and two lovely daughters, she obviously had everything she could wish for.

'So, are we all going to see you off on the afternoon boat to Rhodes?' Francesca said.

Sara smiled happily. 'I hope so. Demetrius picked us up this morning and our luggage is in the back of his car. Francesca, I'd like to ask you a favour. Would you keep an eye on our house while we're away?'

'Of course.'

The conversation around the two sisters was flowing noisily. Nobody was listening to them. Sara leaned across and lowered her voice.

'You may want to use it as a hide-away house, Francesca. When you've been independent for so long, family life could be a bit overwhelming. Please, feel free to move in if you want to and treat it like home. I'll give you a key.'

Francesca smiled. 'You understand me so well, Sara.'

Aware that she'd been ignoring Sotiris, who was sitting next to her, she turned to him and said, 'Michaelis is lucky that you were free to take his place for three months.'

Sotiris hesitated. The least explanation here would be the best thing. 'I happened to meet Michaelis at a conference in Athens some time ago. I told him that if the opportunity arose for me to take a temporary job on Ceres I would like to take it. I don't see enough of my family here.'

'You still have family on Ceres?'

'Yes.'

Francesca waited for Sotiris to elaborate but no further information was forthcoming. Her father was serving lamb from the large roast that had been cooked on the charcoal grill outside the kitchen door. Vegetables, fresh from the garden this morning, were being passed around—courgettes, baby carrots, lightly cooked spinach and roast potatoes.

Sotiris was talking to Chloe and Demetrius now, asking them about their house in the upper town. Francesca gathered that Sotiris was living in the upper town, too. She couldn't help wondering if he was living alone while he was here. Perhaps he'd brought a wife or girlfriend with him. Somehow, she felt she would be intruding if she asked.

And, anyway, why did she want to know? Why was she so drawn towards him? He'd made it quite clear that he didn't want to get to know her. Beyond their work at the hospital, they had nothing in common.

Francesca began to chat with Andonis, seated on her other side, about procedures at the hospital. Now, here was a nice helpful doctor!

'Like I said, Francesca, you'll soon get used to working at the hospital. And if there's anything you want to know while you're on duty, just call me. I've been working here for ever so I can point you in the right direction if you've got a problem.'

'Thanks, Andonis.'

Francesca stood up and gathered the plates to take to the kitchen. Sara and Chloe followed her, returning with bowls of figs, dishes of Greek yoghurt and plates of oranges.

Anthony glanced at the clock and suggested that they mustn't linger over the dessert course if they were to be in time for the ferry.

As everybody was leaving the table Sotiris said he wouldn't be able to join the farewell group in the harbour.

'I have to get back,' he said. 'Thank you so much for your hospitality. I hope you have a wonderful honeymoon, Michaelis and Sara. I'm looking forward to working with my colleagues at the hospital.'

He gave a brief smile to the assembled group before making his way outside.

Francesca hurried to her bedroom and went out onto the terrace. Sotiris was climbing into his car. Like most people on the island, he'd chosen a sturdy four-wheel-drive as the roads were bumpy and difficult to negotiate. For an instant, Sotiris glanced up. It was too late for Francesca to go back inside. He'd seen her.

He smiled and waved a hand. Her heart lifted. She raised her hand in response. He closed the car door and started the engine. She remained watching as Sotiris drove off, leaving a cloud of dust and gravel in his wake.

Turning back inside, she felt a definite sense of loss. She'd actually hoped Sotiris would be staying with the party this afternoon. What was so important that he had to get back? Or, rather, who was so important?

As Sotiris drove carefully along the narrow track that led around the bay of Nimborio to Ceres town he was wishing he could have stayed longer with the Metcalfe family. More especially with Francesca. He'd felt a deep attraction towards her, even though it would be stupid to pursue his feelings any further than being a casual friend.

Driving slowly along the crowded harbourside, he found himself still thinking about her. But this was how he'd felt when he first met Sophia. It had taken him longer to discover what Sophia was really like, whereas Francesca had been more open about what sort of woman she was.

It was a relief to get through the town and be able to drive at a decent speed up the winding metalled road that led to the upper town. On his right-hand side was the steep, sparsely grassed hillside, to his left the beautiful, impressive view of Ceres town and harbour. The scent of the herbs from the hills wafted in through his open window. A goat came careering onto the road and he stopped to let it cross to continue its hurtling descent towards the sea.

Waiting for the goat to disappear, he found he still couldn't get Francesca out of his mind. But he would have to! He couldn't afford to make the same mistake twice. Anyway, she was the sort of fiery, spirited woman who would probably turn him down even if he plucked up courage to ask her out.

In the upper town he drove slowly along the ancient narrow streets until he reached his house. The door opened even before he'd climbed out of the car and Alexander came rushing out, his little arms outspread in welcome.

'Daddy, Daddy, you're home!'

As Sotiris picked up his son and hugged him closely, he found himself wondering how any woman would want to deny herself the indescribable joy of having a child.

CHAPTER TWO

SOTIRIS had called a meeting of all the medical staff at the hospital and Francesca could tell he was nervous. Well, so would she have been if she'd been suddenly plunged into the position of medical director. A newcomer like herself, she knew how he must be feeling, having to take charge of so many people who'd worked here a long time.

From her position at the back of the staff dining room where the chairs and tables had been pushed back to allow more space, Francesca looked around her at the doctors and nurses who'd left their work for a few minutes to listen to what Sotiris had to stay. She estimated there were about thirty people. They were a mixture of Greek, English and Australian staff so Sotiris spoke mostly in English.

A few medical staff had been left to take care of the patients for the duration of this meeting, Sotiris had explained, saying that he was going to be necessarily brief so that the hospital could return to normal as quickly as possible.

He didn't want to radically change anything while Michaelis was away. There were a few other points on which he elaborated before asking for questions from the floor. Nearing the end of the meeting now, Sotiris had reverted to Greek to explain something in answer to a question about off-duty from a young Greek nurse.

Francesca found she could follow the gist of what he was saying but she knew she was going to have to work on her spoken and written Greek. Apparently, the off-duty rota would be the responsibility of the nursing sister in charge of the section of the hospital where the nurse was working. In the case of the doctors, Sotiris would continue to organise that as Michaelis had done. But being a new boy—this description of himself got a much-needed laugh from his audience, Francesca noticed—he would take advice from doctors who'd been at the hospital longer than he had.

'Isn't it going to be a bit of a change from being an important consultant in a big Athens hospital?' one young doctor called out, in what Francesca thought sounded like a cheeky voice. 'I mean won't you find it boring to be stuck on this small back-of-beyond island where even the plumbing doesn't work properly?'

Sotiris smiled. 'I was born on this back-of-beyond island. My family still live here. Do you know Constantinos Street in Chorio? My father, Constantinos Popadopoulos, rebuilt all the houses on that street that had suffered bomb damage during the Second World War. That's where I was born and that's where I live now. I was helping my father to plumb in new lavatories and pipes while you were still in primary school.'

Francesca noticed the room had gone quiet. You would have been able to hear the proverbial pin drop as Sotiris drew himself to his full height and moved forward towards the staff in the front row.

'Yes, it's going to be a change for me, but a change for the better. I've wanted to come home for a long time,' Sotiris said, his voice husky. 'Now I've finally made it, and with your help I'm hoping to keep this hospital running smoothly. So, please, come and see me if you've any problems, any suggestions, any advice.'

There was a murmur of approval. Francesca could feel her colleagues warming to this unknown man. Michaelis had told her that a number of doctors had approached him, asking if they could take over the post of medical director while he was away. But he'd felt that appointing someone from inside would cause too much dissension amongst them and, besides, Michaelis had assured her, Sotiris was far and away the best man for the job.

There were a couple more questions for Sotiris to answer before Francesca realised he was looking over the heads of the people at the front, directly at her.

'I'd like to introduce our newest member of staff to you,' Sotiris was now saying in English. 'Dr Francesca Metcalfe has joined us temporarily. Francesca is a paediatric registrar in a London hospital and...Francesca, if you wouldn't mind raising your hand so that everybody can see you...'

Francesca could feel her lips quivering as she forced a smile and looked around the sea of faces now turned towards her. Some staff smiled back, others didn't. She wasn't normally a shy person but this morning she didn't feel at ease. Her sister Chloe, who was the nursing sister in charge of the whole of the surgical floor, had elected to stay behind at her post. A smile from her sister would have been reassuring at this moment. But there was Andonis, the kindly doctor who'd come to lunch yesterday, beaming at her nearby.

As she was leaving the room a little later, she felt a hand on her arm.

'Francesca, if you wouldn't mind seeing me for a few minutes in my office...'

She followed Sotiris along the corridor to the door marked MEDICAL DIRECTOR.

'Coffee?' Sotiris picked up the cafetière on his desk.

'Oh, yes, please.' Francesca sank down into an armchair at the side of Sotiris's desk. 'It was something of an ordeal to have to meet all my colleagues so early in the morning.'

Sotiris smiled as he handed over a cup of strong black coffee. 'For me, too, but I thought I'd throw us both in at the deep end. How do you think the meeting went?'

'Very well, once you'd thawed everybody out. That was a good idea to tell them about your background here on the island. Do the Popadopoulos family own the whole of Constantinos Street?'

'Yes, we're a big family, all in different houses, but our doors are always open so we wander between them. I used to love that when I was a small child, being spoiled by my aunts and my grandparents.'

Francesca took a sip of her coffee. The caffeine taste hit the back of her throat. She put the cup down on the desk as she leaned forward, placing her hands on the desk as she watched the endearingly animated expression on Sotiris's face as he talked about his family.

Through the open window she could see down to the fascinating, picturesque harbour, the boats coming and going, everybody busy with their morning tasks. Fish were being unloaded, a man was cleaning crabs. Restaurant and taverna workers, haggling about prices, squatted on their heels at the edge of the water. For a moment she could imagine Sotiris as a small boy running along the quayside just as that little suntanned, dark-haired boy down there was doing. What a great island to grow up on!

'Are your parents still alive?' she asked.

'My father died last year, but my mother is still very much alive, very much in charge of the family.'

'I'm so sorry to hear about your father, Sotiris,' Francesca said gently. 'It must be a great comfort that your mother is with you. It's good being part of a big family, isn't it? I often think that although I won't marry and have children of my own…' She paused as she saw the pitying expression on Sotiris's face. 'I'm always part of the Metcalfe family,' she finished, unable to keep the emotional longing from her voice.

Drawn by the warmth in Francesca's voice, Sotiris leaned across the desk and put a hand over hers. She didn't move. Her hand felt warm, soft and very small.

After a few moments of sheer indulgence, he drew back his hand. He'd wanted to make physical contact with Francesca ever since he'd met her yesterday, but this wasn't the time or the place to give way to his fanciful thoughts. Looking at her now, he could see that her eyes were still calm and expressive. The physical contact hadn't touched her as emotionally as it had moved him. Good! She'd taken it as a friendly gesture.

'Well we can't talk about family all day,' he said, trying to revert to a professional-type voice. 'Basically, as a doctor here, you'll be expected to work in the emergency area for part of the day. During the summer months we always have a stream of tourists coming in with injuries. After you've seen and treated them, you either let them go away, if they're fit enough, or admit them to the appropriate ward if they need further treatment. You're expected to follow up the cases you admit.'

Francesca nodded. 'Fine!'

'But I want to make full use of your skills as a paediatrician. So when you're not needed elsewhere, please, work with the patients on the children's ward. And you'll probably find that the nursing staff will bleep you for help in Paediatrics even when you're working somewhere else. This morning we've got a sick children's clinic. They may or may not have seen one of the Ceres doctors before they come to hospital. I'd like you to be there from the start in...' he glanced at his watch '...half an hour.'

Francesca smiled. 'That sounds like my kind of job.' She stood up.

Sotiris came round the desk and stood next to her. There was a hint of some enticingly arousing scent coming from her blonde hair, or maybe it was her skin. Somewhere near the nape of her neck perhaps. He suppressed a shiver. She'd put a white coat over a very attractive flimsy summer dress but it didn't cover her beautiful, slim yet curvaceous figure.

Francesca was unnerved by the closeness of Sotiris. Unnerved in the most exciting way. Yesterday she'd wondered if he was handsome. Today she had no doubt about his good looks. That chiselled jaw, the dark suntanned skin, the strong white teeth. When he smiled at her as he was doing now, she experienced a sort of tingling feeling running down her spine.

It wasn't an entirely new experience for her. She'd been there before and knew what symptom this was the start of! The diagnosis was obvious. If she hadn't been fighting the feeling she would have surmised she was falling for this man.

'There's just one more thing, Francesca. I was wondering...'

Sotiris paused as he dared to put a hand on Francesca's shoulder. He'd tried to make it seem nonchalantly natural, but how unprofessional could he get?

He really should get a grip on himself. What he really wanted to do now was pull this delightful girl into his arms. No strings attached. Simply to hold her and...

'Yes?'

Francesca's beautiful wide blue eyes were staring up at him, waiting for him to finish the sentence he'd started.

He cleared his throat. 'I was wondering if you would like to have a drink with me when we come off duty this evening. It would be nice to discuss how we survived our first day at the hospital over a drink at one of the tavernas in the harbour.'

She remained impassively noncommittal as she considered the idea.

Watching her now, Sotiris was sure she was going to turn him down. The phone rang. He was glad of the interruption as he turned back to his desk.

'I'd like that,' Francesca said quietly.

He answered the phone. '*Sotiris Popadopoulos. Parakalor, imme—*' He broke off and put his hand over the mouthpiece. Francesca was opening the door to leave. Had he heard her right? Had she said...?

'Francesca!'

She was smiling. 'See you later.'

She closed the door and for a moment leaned against it. Phew! She simply didn't know what to make of Sotiris. He seemed to blow hot and cold with her. One minute she thought he disapproved of her, the next he seemed to like her a lot. She'd enjoyed the touch of his hand on hers, the feel of his fingers on her shoulder. Mmm! A delicious shiver of excitement ran through her.

Yes, it would be great to meet him for a drink this evening, but she hoped he wouldn't want to talk shop all the time! A little romance would be nice, a mild flirtation, nothing more...that was, unless he was married.

Hmm, was this just a drink after work before he went home to little wifey up in the Popadopoulos colony? Oh, dear, she wished she'd had the nerve to check that out before she'd got herself all excited. Married men were a definite no-no. She'd have to find out in the first few minutes this evening and beat a hasty retreat if her fears were true.

As she walked along, following the signs to the main entrance of the hospital, Francesca was warming to the place. It seemed such a dear little hospital after the anonymous atmosphere of the huge London hospital where she'd worked. Everyone she came in contact with seemed happy to be working here.

She reached the reception desk. 'I'm Francesca Metcalfe. I know it's not a very big hospital but my sister Chloe told me you would give me a plan of the various departments. You're Michelle, aren't you?'

The Australian receptionist smiled as she handed over a small booklet. 'I certainly am. There you go, Doctor. Chloe told me to expect you. Any time you need help in finding things, just call and see me. This is the reception area, of course, and the emergency area leads off through that door over there. That other door leads to Outpatients.'

Francesca was looking down at her plan. 'I can see that the theatre block is further along and the children's ward, still on the ground floor, is at the back.'

'Yes, that's so the children can play in the garden when they're fit enough. Upstairs are the wards. Your sister's in charge of the first-floor surgical wards—Obstetrics, Gynaecology, General Surgery,

Orthopaedics. Each ward has its own sister but Chloe has overall charge of them.'

Francesca smiled. 'I'm very impressed with my little sister.'

'We all are. And she looks after her twins when she's off duty, doesn't she?'

'She certainly does. Thanks for your help, Michelle.'

A helpful nurse was waiting for her in Outpatients, pointing her towards the desk where she would sit for consultations. A pile of case notes stood at the edge of the desk. A computer was on a separate desk.

The patients were sitting in a bay around the corner. The nurse called the first one in. Such a dear little boy! But he looked pale and nervous. Francesca went round her desk to welcome him and his mother, trying to put them at their ease. She never liked to keep a desk between herself and the patient.

'Do sit down,' she said to the mother. 'I'm Dr Francesca. Now, how can I help you?'

'My boy...his nose...' the mother began in halting English.

Francesca leaned forward. '*Parakalor*, please, speak in Greek if that is easier for you.'

The mother smiled and began again. Francesca concentrated hard. Yes, she understood what was being said. She was also making her own appraisal of the young boy and in her estimation he was very sick.

It transpired that the mother had brought her eight-year-old son, Makis, into the hospital this morning because he was always having nosebleeds. When questioned further, the mother admitted that he'd also had some bleeding from the mouth on occasions and once or twice there had been blood in his little trousers.

Francesca took the little boy into a cubicle and

hoisted him up onto the examination couch. The mother sat on a chair, watching. During her full and thorough examination of young Makis, Francesca discovered small blood-like spots on his legs and in his mouth. Palpating the left side of his abdomen, she could feel that the spleen was definitely enlarged. The boy looked very thin.

'I have kept him home from school since Easter,' the mother said. 'He was always tired.'

'Does Makis sleep well at night?'

The mother shook her head. 'He gets very hot. Sometimes he sweats so much I have to change the sheets.'

'Did you take him to the doctor?'

Makis's mother hesitated. 'I am bringing him to see you now. I have been very busy with my other four children. I never had to take any of them to the doctor, so I thought that Makis would soon be well again.'

'I want to do some medical tests on Makis,' Francesca explained. 'I'm afraid I'll have to keep him in the hospital.'

'Can't you give him some medicine to make him better at home?' the mother asked in surprise.

'I'm sorry, but no. Your son needs hospital care.'

The mother's eyes filled with tears. 'You will take good care of my Makis.'

'Of course.' Francesca smiled reassuringly at the anxious mother. 'You can stay with Makis here if you like. There are facilities for parents to be with their children.'

The mother shook her head sadly. 'I have four more children, three younger than Makis. I cannot stay here but I will come often.' She leaned down and kissed her small son, who remained impassively staring up at her.

Francesca looked down at the little boy. He was already very weak. She hoped they would be able to arrest the progress of the disease. He was displaying some of the classic symptoms of leukaemia but she would need to do a series of tests to be sure. She mustn't jump to conclusions before she'd investigated thoroughly. But the small blood-like spots certainly had the appearance of petechiae, found in leukaemia. And the enlarged spleen was another telling sign.

Having reassured Makis's mother and arranged for the admission of her young patient to the paediatric ward, Francesca carried on seeing the rest of her patients. There was the usual variety of childhood ailments. Most children were allowed home after treatment but she had to admit Costas, a little seven-year-old boy with acute appendicitis, who had been sent through to her clinic from the emergency area.

Costas had clung to his mother when Francesca had tried to examine his painful abdomen. Gradually, she'd been able to coax him to lie still and trust her. It had taken a lot of patience, but Francesca never appeared to hurry when she was caring for young, frightened children who were in obvious pain. It had taken only a few moments of palpating the right iliac fossa to feel the rigidity and the obvious signs that the appendix was inflamed.

Checking with Theatre about the possibility of an emergency operation, she was surprised to find herself talking to Sotiris.

'Yes, I'll fit your patient in this morning, Francesca,' he said easily. 'I was just about to scrub up and get started on my list.'

'I'm glad you're keeping your hand in. I'd hate to

think of your talents going to waste while you sit at a desk.'

'No chance of that. I told Michaelis that I wanted to remain a hands-on doctor. I've delegated all the paperwork to my secretary. Now, about your patient. Has he had anything to eat or drink in the last few hours?'

'No, his mother, very sensibly, thought he might need surgery so he hasn't eaten or drunk anything since last night. He's in considerable pain so...'

'I'll put him first on my list.'

'Thanks, Sotiris.'

As she put down the phone, Francesca was thinking how good it was to be working in a small hospital, where everybody appeared to pull together. It was unlikely a surgeon would ever answer the phone just before beginning his surgical list in the hospital where she'd been working. It was good to know she was handing over Costas to a dedicated, experienced surgeon who was going to operate before the appendix ruptured.

Another disturbing case presented itself at the end of the morning clinic. A little English girl with a rash near the hairline and behind the ears was brought in by her mother.

'Julie's had a cold for a few days, Doctor, but, being on holiday here, we just tried to ignore it. Anyway, last night she was so hot—I didn't have a thermometer with me but I'm sure she had a temperature.'

'You were right,' Francesca said, looking at the temperature reading she'd just taken.

She leaned over the little girl to check out the spots. 'How old are you, Julie?'

'Six.'

'You're a big girl for six. Will you open your mouth wide for me, Julie?' Francesca asked gently.

On the mucous surface of the cheek in a line with the upper molars were white spots surrounded by an area of hyperaemia—Koplik's spots, the classic diagnostic symptom of measles.

'When did Julie's spots first appear?'

'I first noticed them yesterday.'

'I'm afraid Julie's got measles. I take it she hasn't been vaccinated against measles?'

The mother frowned. 'I couldn't decide what to do about it. There was all that controversy about which jabs to have. My mother said she'd had measles when she was a child and it hadn't been too bad. Everybody did in those days, didn't they, Doctor? I couldn't make up my mind about it, so I just sort of left it for a bit and…'

Francesca took a deep breath. No point in being controversial at this stage. The child had measles and there was no turning back the clock.

'Have you any other children?'

'No, Julie's our only child.'

'Well, I'll have to admit her to hospital. We don't want the measles to spread to other children. She'll be kept away from the other patients. Would you like to stay here with her? Most children like to have their mother around.'

Julie's mother nodded immediately. 'I'll need to let my husband know where we'll be. How long will we have to stay?'

'About two weeks, until the rash and the cold-like symptoms disappear and we can be sure Julie isn't infectious.'

'Two weeks! But we're due to fly home next week.'

'I'm sorry but that's out of the question with an infectious child. Have you got travel insurance?'

The mother nodded. 'Yes.'

'I'll give you a written statement to say you're unable to fly on the date you booked.'

'Can my husband go back home? He's got a business to run.'

'Of course. Now, as you're my last patient of the day, I'll be able to take you along to the children's ward, Mrs Greenwood.'

'Call me Helen, Doctor. If I'm going to be staying here for a while, I expect we'll be getting to know each other. Can I go back to the hotel for my toiletry things and…?'

Francesca answered all Helen's queries about where she would sleep at the hospital before taking mother and daughter along to the paediatric ward. A small room that looked out over the garden was hastily prepared as an isolation unit for the little girl. A nurse was assigned as special nurse to Julie and Francesca explained that she must adopt all the techniques of barrier nursing. The nurse was to be gowned and masked when she looked after her small patient.

A measles epidemic on the island was the last thing that was needed at the height of the tourist season.

When she was fully satisfied that the nursing staff understood how to take care of Julie, Francesca left the ward and went off to the staff cloakroom. Putting her white coat in the laundry bin, she found the spare dress and undies she'd brought with her that morning. It was a habit she'd adopted in London. You never knew when you would need to change completely from the clothes you'd been working in.

Stepping into the tiny shower cubicle, she washed

off her workaday self before emerging ready for the evening. A shower always helped her to switch off. This was another habit she'd adopted at the end of a long busy day. You had to keep yourself fit and healthy to survive in the medical profession and being able to relax was most important.

Her pulse was definitely racing now and it had nothing to do with the hot water from the shower! Sotiris's phone call to her in Outpatients towards the end of the afternoon had been terse and to the point.

'Come to my office when you're free,' he'd said.

He'd sounded tired, or maybe he was already regretting having asked her to have a drink with him this evening. Maybe he'd phoned home. She still hadn't had time to check out the possibility of a wife. What an awful thought! She'd better stop torturing herself and find out the truth as soon as possible.

Sotiris stood up from his desk when she went in. He smiled, a deliciously welcoming smile, and came round the desk. For an instant she contemplated asking him then and there whether he was married or not. But there would be no harm in having a drink with him. She could finish her drink quickly and then leave if necessary.

'You've changed your dress,' Sotiris said. 'You're in red. This morning you were wearing green.'

'You're very observant. Especially as I was wearing a white coat over my dress.'

'I like to be observant. It's useful when you're a doctor, don't you think? Come on, let's go before somebody calls me back. I've left a competent surgical team on duty but if I'm still in hospital there's always the possibility they'll phone down for some advice. I'd like to have time for a drink with you before I go home.'

Francesca smiled. 'It sounds as if you haven't got much time this evening. If you'd like to leave it…'

'No, please. Let's go.'

As Sotiris drove her down to the harbour, Francesca saw him glance at his watch. Yes, he was in a hurry. This was simply a courtesy drink. There was some reason why he couldn't spend too much time over this drink.

Sotiris parked round the side of a taverna that was right on the waterfront, facing out over the harbour. They sat outside. The punishing heat of the day was subsiding somewhat and down by the water it was pleasantly warm, rather than oppressively hot.

'I'm glad the hospital is air-conditioned,' Francesca said, as she sipped her glass of wine.

Sotiris nodded. 'It would be unbearable to have to work during August if the hospital didn't have air-conditioning. Especially in Theatre. I had a long list today. And then there was this doctor who sent me an emergency patient at the beginning of the morning.'

He gave her a wry grin. 'Completely threw my timing out.'

Francesca leaned forward. 'How did it go with little Costas?'

'I was able to remove his appendix just in time. It was on the verge of bursting. I'm glad you sent him to me so quickly.'

'Even if it threw your timing out?'

'Timing isn't important in hospital.'

Francesca saw Sotiris glance once more at his watch.

'But timing is obviously important when you're off duty,' she said lightly. 'That's the second time you've glanced at your watch in the past ten minutes. Are you sure you shouldn't be somewhere else?'

'No, no! I still haven't switched off from work, that's all.'

Francesca took a deep breath. 'I was just wondering if you'd got somebody waiting for you at home, Sotiris. Are you married?'

She tossed the question out in a casual aside.

A veiled expression crossed his face. 'I was married. My wife died soon after...soon after we were married.'

'I'm sorry...oh, Sotiris I'm so sorry. I had no idea.'

She leaned forward and automatically took hold of his hand in a gesture of comfort. His eyes, when he raised them to her face, were sad, oh, so sad.

'It was four years ago,' he said quietly.

The feel of her hand in his was so comforting. He leaned towards her, placing both his hands around hers as he thought how much he already admired her. At this moment he wanted to pour out his heart to her. Tell her about Alexander, his wonderful son. He would have liked to have drawn her into his life...share Alex with her. Francesca was a natural with children. He'd seen her at work today and she could win them over in a matter of moments.

But he knew he mustn't introduce her to Alex. He must keep them apart. Alex would take a liking to Francesca. She would be like a mother figure to him. But Francesca didn't want to be a mother. And sooner or later she would break both their hearts...

His phone was ringing. 'Sotiris Popadopoulos.'

He switched to rapid Greek. Francesca heard him telling someone called Arwen that he was on his way home.

Sotiris stood up decisively, coming round the table.

'I'm sorry, I've got to go, Francesca. A family matter.'

Francesca stood up. 'That's OK. I understand.'

Sotiris leaned down and briefly touched the side of Francesca's cheek with his lips. Oh, the feel of her skin on his lips! The scent of her hair, the aura of seductive femininity surrounding her. He wanted to stay close, to be with her all evening, all night, holding her in his arms...

She walked with him to the waterside. Twinkling lights were appearing on the hillsides above the harbour. On the yachts in the harbour there were people sipping their evening cocktails. Their evening was just beginning.

'Can I give you a life home?' Sotiris asked.

'No, thank you. Manolis is coming over for me.'

That wasn't strictly true. Before coming off duty, she'd phoned Manolis, who, besides all his other household and garden work, acted as the Metcalfe boatman, to say that she wouldn't need a lift this evening.

'Next time we have a drink together, I'll make sure I'm completely free for the evening,' Sotiris said.

Francesca stared down into the deep water of the harbour. A shoal of fish was swimming near the surface, attracted by the bright lights. Sotiris had said his wife was dead, so who was the mysterious Arwen who'd summoned him home?

'Goodbye, Sotiris.'

As she turned away she saw him hesitating. Was he torn between going back to she-who-must-be-obeyed and staying for a bit of fun with somebody new? Well, that was his problem. She hurried away. Reaching the end of the harbour, she turned and looked back. There was no sight of Sotiris now. She looked up at the twisting road carved out of the hillside that led to Chorio, the upper town.

Constantinos Street. That's where Sotiris lived.

But who lived with him?

CHAPTER THREE

'OF COURSE I don't mind looking after the children!'

Francesca smiled at her mother and sister, wondering why they'd needed to ask.

'It's my day off. I'll be here all day with nothing to do but enjoy myself, so off you two go and buy curtain material and everything else you need in Rhodes.'

'I'd completely forgotten the twins had asked if their friend Natasha could come over to play today,' Chloe said as she pressed down the plunger on the cafetière.

'Natasha is their best friend at school and her mother is so kind. The twins are always going round to Natasha's house to play. They've been telling Natasha about their grandparents' house being so close to the water and planning a day swimming for ages. But I've been so busy with the wedding and settling into the house that—'

'Look, it's no problem, Chloe. You and Mum have been planning this shopping trip all week. And I know you need to buy all sorts of things for the house.'

Chloe smiled. 'Demetrius was born in our house. I don't want to change too much, but things like curtains and cushions, new bedlinen for the girls' beds, that sort of thing.'

Chloe hesitated. 'There's just one more thing I haven't told you. Natasha has asked if she can bring her little brother. He's only four but apparently he's been swimming like a fish since before he could walk.'

'The more, the merrier,' Francesca said easily, as she spread home-made marmalade on home-baked bread.

They were all sitting out on the terrace. It was one of those wonderful August mornings when the sun was already warm but not too hot. The sound of tinkling bells as the goats foraged for food on the hillside above them was the only disturbance in the entire bay. The scent of the herbs was so evocative of the holidays Francesca had spent out here when she'd been a child that she was beginning to feel positively nostalgic about those far-off days when life had always been so easy.

The twins, having had a hasty breakfast, were playing down on the shore waiting for their friends to arrive. Chloe had driven over from her house in the upper town early that morning to have breakfast with the family.

'I just hope it doesn't feel too much like a busman's holiday for you, Francesca,' Chloe said. 'You're mostly dealing with children in hospital all day and then on your day off I ask you to look after mine.'

Francesca smiled. 'Honestly, I shall really enjoy myself. We'll spend most of the day in the water. Manolis has promised to help with the swimming and act as lifeguard and Dad will be here.'

Francesca leaned across the table to pour more coffee for her father who'd been trying to read a recent copy of *The Lancet* whilst keeping half an ear on what the girls had to say in case it was something that he should know.

'Oh, yes, I've promised Rachel and Samantha they can bring their friends out in the boat with me,' Anthony said. 'We've got some spare lifejackets, haven't we, Pam?'

'I'll get them out before I go,' Pam said, beginning to clear the table.

'Leave that, Mum,' Francesca said. 'You'll miss the boat to Rhodes if you don't go soon.'

She was very much looking forward to her day with the children and the sooner her mother and sister left her and her father to get on with it, the better.

Francesca leaned over the wall of the terrace and waved as she watched her mother and sister setting off on their shopping trip. Spending the day shopping in hot, crowded streets wasn't her scene. She hadn't escaped from London to go shopping, she thought as she lifted her face up towards the sun. Bliss! Well, almost bliss. There was still that niggling little problem at the back of her mind.

She'd tried to ignore it, but since her drink with Sotiris last week she'd felt very unsettled. Instead of bringing them closer together, as she'd hoped, that short encounter at the taverna had seemed to drive a wedge between them.

It had been so frustrating! Just when she'd felt her spirits lifting at the thought that Sotiris was a free man, free to have the mild flirtation she would have enjoyed, she'd had her hopes dashed by that phone call from Arwen, whoever Arwen was.

She stood up, giving herself a little shake. She'd simply got to stop thinking about him in that special kind of way. She saw him in hospital and they worked perfectly well together. Apart from that, there was obviously no future. Even if he did ask her out again, she wouldn't go...well, perhaps she might think about it, but...

Maria had arrived on the terrace, carrying a tray. Francesca went across to help her.

The clearing up was almost finished when, through the kitchen window, Francesca saw a car approaching fast along the narrow, dusty road that skirted the bay. Piling the last of the plates near the sink, she went out to greet her little guests.

A tall Greek man was lifting Natasha down from a large four-wheel-drive. A little dark-haired boy was patiently awaiting his turn in the back of the car, peering through the window. Francesca went round and opened the door, holding out her arms towards him.

'I'm Francesca,' she said, gently. '*Posseleni?* What's your name?'

She thought it best to try a mixture of English and Greek with this little boy. So many children spoke English nowadays and she could hear the girls chattering away in English to each other. The Greek children liked to practise their English with English people. A whole generation was now growing up on the island who watched English and American films on television and had excellent language teaching at school.

'I'm Alexander,' the little boy said solemnly, in English. 'But you can call me Alex if you're a friend of my sister, Natasha.'

Francesca lifted Alex down onto the hard gravel in front of the house. He squared his little shoulders and looked up at the unknown lady.

'How old are you, Alex?'

'I'm four and a quarter,' the little boy said proudly.

'You're a big boy. I thought you were nearly five.'

Alex was still holding her hand. Francesca turned to greet the man who'd driven the children to the house. 'You must be Alexander's father.'

'No, I'm Natasha's father, Spiros.' He smiled as he held out his strong, broad hand.

'I'm Francesca, Chloe's sister.'

'I can see the family resemblance. Alex is my nephew, but he's been brought up in our house with his cousins since he was a baby. They regard him as their little brother.'

'That's nice.' Francesca hesitated. The Greeks were always so hospitable whenever she called at someone's house. 'Would you like to come in for a cup of coffee?'

'No, thank you. I must be off. I'm a building contractor and I've got to drive to the other side of the island to check on some work over there. I wonder if you would be able to bring the children home this afternoon? I'll have to work late today and my wife has to go to a governors' meeting at the school.'

Francesca smiled. 'Of course.'

'We live in Chorio, the upper town, not far from Chloe's house. Natasha will show you the way.'

Francesca and the children waved goodbye as the car went back around the bay. The little boy clung tightly to Francesca's hand as the three girls ran, giggling and laughing, onto the shore. The twins were already in their swimsuits and Natasha quickly stripped off to reveal that she was wearing hers under her dress.

Francesca sensed that little Alex was somewhat overawed by being set down in a completely new environment. Poor little mite! She wondered why he'd been brought up with his cousins and what had happened to his parents. If he'd been a patient she would have asked more questions about his background so as to be able to put him at his ease, but in a social situation it was none of her business. She simply knew she wanted to make the day as happy as possible for him.

Manolis had already taken up his position on the

shore, watching the girls like a hawk as they ran shrieking with delight into the water.

'Would you like a drink and a biscuit, Alex?' Francesca said.

The suntanned little face broke into a wide smile that revealed strong white baby teeth and a very healthy pink tongue. Francesca decided she must stop scrutinising the boy as a doctor and simply enjoy taking care of him.

'Yes, please, Fran...Fran... What did you say your name was?'

'Francesca, but you can call me Fran, if you like.'

'No, I can say it now. Francesca. That's a pretty name.'

Together they walked up to the house. In the kitchen Maria fussed over the little boy, piling a plate high with her home-made biscuits while he sat on the floor, happily stroking the cat.

Over at the hospital, Sotiris was just finishing his morning's paperwork. It had to be done before he could escape to the operating theatre and get on with some real work. Panayota, his secretary, was very efficient and helped him enormously, but there were certain clerical duties that only he could perform.

There! He pushed the papers to the other side of the desk. Panayota would deal with the boring stuff. He took a sip of the coffee he'd forgotten to drink. It had gone cold in the air-conditioning. His eyes were drawn to the hot sunny day outside. He would love to be out there on the hills...but not alone.

Since meeting Francesca last week he'd found himself thinking constantly about her. It had been about ten days, actually, but it seemed much longer than that since she'd come into his life. She'd appeared like a ray of sunshine, and what had he done about it? Nothing, absolutely nothing! They'd had a drink together down at the harbour and just when they'd been getting to know each other, his sister had phoned to ask him to bring some bread for supper.

As he'd cut the connection, he'd known by the look on Francesca's face that she'd gone off him. And who could blame her? He'd simply hoped for a light-hearted relationship with her. He couldn't risk anything more. Not with Alex around. Alex didn't want to see his father with someone he would regard as a mother figure, only to have her disappear from their lives.

When he thought of little Alex he felt that warm, loving feeling that kept him happy as a father. This morning Alex had dashed off next door to join his cousins, with his little bag that held his swimming things. Arwen had phoned early this morning to say both Natasha and Alex had been invited to spend the day with some school friends. She'd rung off before he'd had time to ask exactly where Alex was going, but he trusted Arwen's judgement where Alex's welfare was concerned.

Still, it didn't stop him wishing he could spend more time with his son. That was something that Francesca would never have to worry about. But cherishing her family and her little patients was obviously enough for her.

He wasn't even going to see Francesca at the hospital today because she was scheduled for a day off. He should have scheduled a day off for both of them at the same time but he'd thought his intentions might be too obvious. He had to play it cool if he was to regain her confidence. He only wanted to see her again, to take her out and get to know her. Nothing emotionally complicated.

Francesca wouldn't want a serious relationship either. She was married to her career. It was good for the hospital but agony for him when he thought of how wonderful it would be to contemplate the possibility of a serious relationship with her.

The phone on his desk was ringing. He answered, telling the theatre sister he was on his way.

Francesca carried the plate of biscuits on a tray from the kitchen, with a glass of milk for Alex and a cup of coffee for herself. Alex climbed the stairs and trotted behind her until they reached the terrace. Turning to look at him as she pulled chairs to the edge of the terrace, she saw he was utterly relaxed now. It hadn't taken him long to adapt to the new situation.

Alex sat down on a wooden chair, looking out over the bay, his sturdy little legs swinging as he watched Natasha, Rachel and Samantha cavorting in the water. Francesca leaned back in her chair, closing her eyes as she allowed the sun to shine full on her face. This was the sort of little boy she would have loved to have had. She was twenty-nine. If she could have started having babies when she'd finished her medical training, she could have completed her family by now. Three or four would have been nice.

She must stop these useless daydreams! She opened her eyes and saw that Alex was watching her. She leaned forward and held out the plate of biscuits.

Alex smiled as he stretched out his little hand. Francesca could see the baby dimples over his knuckles.

'Did you cook these biscuits?'

Francesca shook her head. 'Maria baked them. Would you like another one?'

'Yes, please.'

As Alex munched happily, he leaned across the table to pick up a book that Rachel had left behind. He flicked through it, looking at some of the pictures.

'This is a bit hard for me to read, Francesca. Will you read it to me?'

'Of course.'

It was a long story, but Francesca knew it wouldn't be a good idea to plunge the little boy into the water too soon after this second breakfast. And secretly she simply wanted to enjoy being with him. The children she cared for in her professional life were usually sick children. Here was a healthy, happy, intelligent young boy so full of life and curiosity that it was a pleasure to spend time with him.

Towards the end of the morning, when they were in the sea, Francesca was astounded at how well all the children could swim. She'd swum with the twins nearly every day since she'd arrived on the island. Their swimming was very good, but they couldn't compete with Natasha and Alex, who were complete naturals in the water.

Apparently, although the family lived in the upper town, they had a beach house on a small island further down the coast where they spent a lot of time in the summer months. Little Alex had been introduced to the water when he'd been only a few months old.

The day passed too quickly for Francesca. She'd wondered earlier if she would have a problem keeping three eight-year-old girls and a four-year-old boy occupied, but it was quite the reverse. When the agreed time for their departure came, she found herself wishing they could stay longer.

They'd had hours of good swimming and a picnic lunch on the shore, followed by a trip in the boat. In the middle of the bay Anthony had given fishing lessons to everybody, which had been hilarious. The sight of little Alex, with a fish dangling on the end of his line, determined to haul it in whilst Anthony held tightly to the little boy to prevent him going overboard, was one of the high spots of the day.

'You'll have to come again,' Francesca told Alex and Natasha as she helped them into the back of her father's car.

'Oh, yes, please!' Alex said.

Natasha smiled. 'I'd love to.'

As she drove along the bayside road, Francesca could see the twins and her father still waving from the house. It had been one of those truly perfect days which she would remember for a long time. Twenty-nine wasn't exactly old, but she'd felt as if she'd been as young as the children today.

She craned her neck to get a better view of little Alex in her rear-view mirror. He was sucking his thumb, curled up in a little ball. She'd strapped him in securely with the seat belt and a booster cushion, but he'd somehow managed, in spite of the harness, to make himself as relaxed as only small children could.

Natasha, by contrast, chatted continually in a happy, excited voice. 'It's been great, Francesca! Will you be here when we come again?'

'I'll try to be, Natasha. If I'm not working. Now, you'll have to tell me the way to your house.'

They were driving up the winding road to Chorio, a

sheer drop to the sea on one side and the steep hillside on the other.

'Take the road into the village at the top of the hill and then I'll show you the way. The streets are a bit narrow but it's quite easy when you've done it a few times,' Natasha said, in a grown-up voice. 'There…over there, good, now take that left turning…slow down because it's going to get even narrower…'

This street was intriguing. It turned from the main thoroughfare of the village and if Francesca hadn't known it was here she would have driven straight past it. At the beginning of the street and along the sides there were large tubs of geraniums. The houses were ancient but very well preserved. Probably rebuilt houses from a bygone era, but beautifully executed.

Francesca smiled. 'I'm glad I've got a good navigator, Natasha. This is a lovely street, so picturesque.'

'My grandfather rebuilt all these houses before I was born,' Natasha said, proudly. 'This street is where all my family live.'

Something was ringing a bell at the back of her mind but Francesca was too busy to follow it up as she negotiated the narrow street, past the tubs of flowers, the ancient stone statues, the wrought-iron lamps and a tabby cat snoozing in the sun. It was like moving back into history, but with all the added advantages of the twenty-first century.

One of the most wonderful things about the street was that all the doors were wide open, displaying the beautifully refurbished interiors. Talk about a welcoming ambience! Where else in the world would she ever see such a delightful street?

'That's my house!' Natasha shouted excitedly.

Francesca brought the car to a halt, jumped out and opened the back passenger doors to help the children out.

'Mummy, we've had a great time!' Natasha was shouting in Greek. 'Where are you, Mummy?'

A boy of about ten came out of the house.

'Where's Mum, Lefteris?'

'She's not back yet.'

'Thanks for a brilliant day, Francesca!'

Natasha ran in through the open door. Alex, still semi-slumbering, tightened his arms around Francesca's neck as she undid the seat belt and lifted him out. She held him close, preparing to follow Natasha into the house.

A man was coming out of the house next door.

'Francesca!'

'Sotiris!'

Alex opened his eyes and, immediately awake, released himself from Francesca to dash forward into Sotiris's arms.

'Daddy! Daddy!'

Over the top of his son's head, Sotiris looked at Francesca.

'This is Francesca, Daddy. She's been looking after me all day and we've had a lovely time. I caught a fish and Francesca's girls helped me to put it back in the water. They'd already got enough fish for their supper.'

'Sounds as if you've had a wonderful day, Alex,' Sotiris said, trying desperately to make sense of the situation. He turned to Francesca. 'Would you like to come in for a drink, Francesca?'

'Oh, yes, please, come into our house, Francesca!' Alex said excitedly. 'Daddy's got some crisps and nuts and beer and…'

Alex dashed ahead into the house.

Sotiris drew in his breath. This was the one thing he'd hoped wouldn't happen. His son had met Francesca and had obviously become besotted by her. Well, who wouldn't? He'd planned to keep them apart. He wanted to see more of Francesca himself, but he didn't want Alex to become involved. When the time came for them to stop seeing each other, Alex would be an innocent casualty.

Even as he was showing Francesca in through the door, Sotiris knew he was asking for trouble. He ought to knock this thing on the head here and now. Be strong about it. But the thought of spending some time with Francesca in an off-duty situation was too much to resist.

'What a lovely house!'

Francesca was looking admiringly round the living room which led out onto a terrace.

They'd walked through a stone-flagged courtyard, fragrant with the scent of the roses that clung to the ancient stone walls. The living room was comfortable, cosy, inviting. Bookshelves lined the walls; deep squashy chairs positively beckoned to be lounged in. But it was the magnificent view from the terrace that drew Francesca through the wide floor-to-ceiling windows, with dark red curtains held back by ribbons, to the terrace beyond.

Wide hills swept down to the sea below them. A white church on the hillside stood out in the magical evening light as the sun dipped low in the sky. Below the church she could just distinguish Sara's and Michaelis's house, partly obscured by the tall fir trees that surrounded it. It reminded her that she must make time to go there again soon to see that everything was OK.

She'd made a couple of trips to the house since her sister had gone on honeymoon and she was enchanted with the place. Use it as a hide-away, Sara had told her, and Francesca knew she would definitely take her sister up on the offer at some point.

Alex had already left Sotiris to take hold of Francesca's hand.

'Sit here, Francesca,' the little boy said, patting a large wicker armchair with deep, squashy cushions.

As soon as she was seated the little boy climbed onto her lap.

Sotiris watched the touching scene with mixed emotions churning inside him. Alex already adored Francesca. How had it happened that the two had spent the day together without him knowing about it? And what was it that Alex had said about Francesca's girls?

'Alex said he'd spent the day with you and your girls,' Sotiris said, leaning against the table on the terrace. 'I didn't know...'

'Rachel and Samantha, Chloe's children, my nieces.' Francesca smiled. 'You didn't think they were mine, did you?'

'No, of course not. Not a dedicated career-woman like you.'

Francesca gave him a brittle smile. It was a bit difficult to keep up the pretence with Sotiris's little boy curled up on her lap like this.

'Exactly! No, as you know, I haven't got any children, Sotiris. I didn't know you had a son. I'm surprised you haven't spoken about Alex before. I would have thought you'd have been so proud of him.'

'Of course I'm proud of him,' Sotiris said quickly.

'I just never got around to mentioning him before. What would you like to drink—wine, beer, ouzo, fruit juice…?'

'I'd better have a fruit juice or something non-alcoholic if I'm to drive my father's car back to Nimborio.'

'Of course. I've got some oranges from the trees in the garden. It won't take a minute in the juicer.'

Sotiris was being terribly polite but Francesca had the distinct feeling he was worried about something. Something to do with the fact that she was here in the house. Perhaps the mysterious Arwen was due to arrive.

She took a sip of the freshly squeezed orange juice Sotiris brought her and nibbled on the crisp that Alex was holding up to her mouth.

'I thought Alex was Natasha's little brother when they first arrived but…'

'Ah, yes, you see, Arwen brought up the cousins together when I was in Athens.'

'Arwen?' Francesca found she was holding her breath.

'My sister. It's a long story.'

Sotiris glanced meaningfully at Alex. Francesca got the message. Not in front of the child. She had the distinct impression that Sotiris was holding something back. Or was it that he simply didn't want her to be there? He was merely being polite because she'd been looking after his son all day. Yes, that was it.

She quickly finished her glass and set it down on the table. 'Thank you. That was delicious. Most refreshing.'

They were like strangers…well, they hadn't known each other very long. Francesca had read more into their earlier encounters than had actually been there. Sotiris was a widower with a child. He had a busy life with his large extended family which didn't include her. Their only point of contact should be at the hospital.

She tried to lift Alex from her lap but he clung firmly to her.

'Don't go, Francesca,' the little boy said. 'Stay and have supper with us.'

'I'm sorry, Alex, I can't. I have to get back to Rebecca and Samantha.'

The look of disappointment on Alex's face was too poignant. Francesca turned to look up at Sotiris who had very firmly lifted Alex from her lap and was now holding him in his arms.

'Can I go and see Grandma, Daddy?'

'Just for a little while,' Sotiris said, gently, as he put Alex down on the floor.

'Bye, Daddy, bye, Francesca. See you soon.' Alex scampered off through the door.

Sotiris was staring down at her with soulful eyes. As he'd lifted his son away, his hands had briefly touched Francesca's bare arm. She had felt a frisson of excitement running through her. There was nothing in the world she would have liked better than to stay here in this lovely house and have supper with Sotiris and Alex.

She stood up determinedly. Daydreams were for children so she was going to be very grown-up about this.

For a moment she thought she was dreaming. Sotiris had put one hand on the back of her head and caressed her hair. She raised her eyes to his.

'I wish you could stay, Francesca,' he said, his voice husky with emotion. 'But I know...'

'I'd love to stay but I promised...'

She broke off. Sotiris was so close, so tantalisingly close. His lips looked so sexy, so seductive. She felt a sensual shiver of excitement running down her spine. It would be so easy to raise her lips towards his... In that instant she felt sure it was what they both wanted but...

With an effort she moved backwards, turning immediately to head for the door.

'I have to go,' she said firmly.

Sotiris remained still and passive as Francesca drove away. Mixed with his sadness was the relief that he'd been able to overcome that brief moment of madness when Francesca had been so close to him.

He'd almost blown his cover. Almost shown his true feelings for her. And he must never do that. If there was to be any relationship at all with this impossibly desirable, totally dedicated career-woman, it had to be a mere light hearted, no-strings-attached affair. Something that both of them would enjoy, that neither of them would regret when it had to end.

And Alex must have no part in this. He loved his son too dearly to have him involved in a situation that could be hurtful to him. If Francesca had been the marrying kind, the situation would have been completely different. She would have been ideal.

Sotiris raised his hand to his face to catch the aroma of the scent that Francesca had been wearing. He was sure it was still lingering there from that brief touch on her arm that had threatened to totally unnerve him. Or perhaps he was merely imagining it. Whatever! It was highly exciting...and deeply frustrating!

It was going to be difficult to relax this evening after he'd put Alex to bed. Not to mention trying to sleep later. When was he going to see Francesca again? Tomorrow at the hospital.

It was going to be a long night.

'Sotiris!' someone called.

'Yassoo, Arwen!'

Sotiris's sister smiled as she walked in through the open door. 'Was that Chloe driving away just now? I wanted to talk to her about some school business that came up at the governors' meeting, but I've only just got back.'

'No, that was her sister, Francesca.'

'Pretty name.' Arwen's eyes narrowed as she looked up at her brother. 'That wasn't the Francesca you had a drink with, was it?'

'My, you've got a good memory! Over a week ago I have a drink on the way home with a new colleague and suddenly it becomes an important event.'

'I didn't say it was an important event, did I? It was just that you seemed a bit edgy when you got home. And ever since...well, I just wondered when you were planning on taking her out again. If she's as nice as her sister she—'

'Don't start matchmaking, Arwen. Francesca has made it quite clear she doesn't want to get married...ever! She's an excellent doctor, totally dedicated to her career.'

Arwen frowned. 'Well, you'd better steer clear of her in that case. We wouldn't want Alex to think Daddy's girlfriend was going to be his new mother, would we?'

Sotiris gave an exasperated sigh. 'Don't you think I've already reasoned that out for myself?'

'No need to get cross with me, Sotiris, I only want what's best for you and Alex. You're my younger brother and I've always worried about you. You've had one disastrous marriage. Don't go getting yourself into hot water again... Now, I came to see if you and Alex are having supper with us tonight.'

'Why don't you come to us for a change? I've promised Alex moussaka and it's already prepared. There'll be enough for everybody.'

'Including Mother?'

'Of course! When does Mother ever have to cook in the evening? Will you go and bring her along, Arwen? Alex is with her, so would bring him home?'

Sotiris went into the kitchen and switched on the oven. At least being surrounded by his family would help to take his mind off Francesca.

As she drove down the winding road that led to the harbour, Francesca was reviewing the situation. In the short time she'd known Sotiris she'd come to like him enormously. More than like. Something akin to falling in love. When she was near him, he affected her in a disastrously disturbing way...

Oops! She swerved to avoid a stray goat that broke into a run. She must give this road all her concentration. The sheer drop on her right-hand side was now illuminated with the lights from the harbour where the water now carried an iridescent sheen. But she mustn't admire the view until she was safely down in the lower town.

She drove carefully round the harbour and made for final stretch of road that led to her home. Going home was nice, but she would have preferred to have spent the evening up there in that cosy house with Sotiris and Alex.

CHAPTER FOUR

FRANCESCA leaned over her little patient as she prepared to take a bone-marrow sample from the back of his hipbone.

'Are you OK, Makis?'

The little boy moved his head against the pillow. 'I'm fine, Francesca. I can't feel anything. Have you stuck the needle in yet?'

'This little scratchy feeling…that was the needle going in… You'll feel a bit numb around your back soon… And now I'm taking the sample I told you about…'

'It sort of tickles…now it's hurting a bit, sort of…' Makis drew in his breath. 'Now it's OK again.'

'You're a good boy, Makis,' Francesca said, as she withdrew the syringe containing the bone-marrow sample. 'You can move again now.'

Makis looked up at Francesca enquiringly. 'Is that all? It didn't take long, did it? What are you going to do with the stuff in that syringe?'

'I'm going to send it down to the laboratory where they will look at it and find out what kind of treatment you'll need to make you feel better.'

'What do you think is wrong with me, Francesca?'

Francesca hesitated. This was the question she'd dreaded. How do you tell an eight-year-old you think he might have leukaemia? He wouldn't know what leukaemia was, so she'd then have to explain it as simply as possible. And then again to his mum.

She didn't have to tell him until the results came from the laboratory. She just had to reassure him that they were doing everything they could to make him comfortable. Nothing was conclusive yet, but from the recent blood tests where leukaemia cells were present it only needed the bone-marrow sample to confirm the diagnosis.

'As soon as we get the report from the laboratory I'll come and chat to you and your mother,' Francesca said. 'You've been a really good boy and now I'd like you to have a little rest. I'll come back and see you later.'

She ruffled Makis's hair in an affectionate gesture. The little boy caught hold of her hand.

'I'm glad you're my doctor, Francesca. I used to be scared of doctors but you're sort of like...well, like a mum, really.'

Francesca smiled. 'That's one of the nicest things anybody's said to me in a long time, Makis.'

She turned as somebody came in through the curtains she'd pulled round Makis's bed. It was Sotiris, wearing theatre greens.

'Sister told me you were here, Francesca. Could you check out young Costas for me? I'm a bit rushed this morning. Been in Theatre since the early hours.'

'Of course I'll check on Costas.'

'Thanks.' Sotiris hesitated. 'I need to talk to you, Francesca, when you've finished. My office about twelve?'

'Anything in particular?'

'Can't talk now. I'm on my way from Theatre to see an emergency patient I operated on early this morning. I thought it would be easier to call in here and see you on my way, delegate some of my work and have a look at Makis. That looks like the bone-marrow sample we're waiting for. I'll drop it into the lab when I'm going past. The sooner we get the results back...'

Sotiris broke off as he moved nearer to their young patient. 'How are you feeling now, Makis?'

Makis grinned. 'I'm OK. Francesca didn't hurt me. I knew she wouldn't because she's a good doctor, isn't she?'

'She certainly is.' Sotiris squeezed Makis's hand. 'And you're a good patient.'

'I like being here in the children's ward but I'd really like to go home to my brothers and sister. How long will it be before you can make me better?'

Francesca looked across the bed at Sotiris and saw her own anxiety mirrored in his eyes.

'We can't make you better quickly, Makis,' Sotiris said gently. 'It's going to take some time so, you're going to have to be very patient. We'll be able to give you more idea of what's happening when we get the results of this test.'

As soon as Sotiris had gone, Francesca made Makis comfortable before leaving him to have a snooze. She'd given him a mild sedative before starting the procedure and it had taken effect, helping to ease away the discomfort.

She still had to check on her other little patients. She soon found that Costas, the boy who Sotiris had asked her to see, was now fit. In fact he was running around the garden laughing and shouting with a couple of other patients who had made good recoveries from their operations of the previous week.

'Nothing much wrong with you, Costas,' Francesca said, when she'd managed to catch her young patient and get him to lie still on his bed for a few moments while she examined him.

The wound was healing nicely, the stitches were out and Costas was obviously in good health again.

'Would you like to go home, Costas?'

'Yes, please!'

'I'll have a word with Dr Sotiris when I see him.'

Her final patient, Julie, was still being barrier nursed in a side ward. The measles rash had mostly disappeared. Francesca listened to Julie's chest. Clear as a whistle. Fortunately, there had been no serious complications and the initial cold-like symptoms and cough had disappeared.

'We'll give it a few more days, Helen,' Francesca said to Julie's mother, as she folded up her stethoscope and put it into the pocket of her white coat. When the rash has completely gone, we can consider Julie to be not infectious so you could book seats on a plane for the end of next week. Your husband's already gone, hasn't he?'

'Yes, he went back a few days after we came in here. He had to get back to work. It'll be great to be all together again as a family.'

'It's not been easy for you, Helen. But you've been a great help to all of us.'

Julie's mother smiled. 'Well, you've all been so good to Julie. Especially at the beginning when she was feverish.'

Francesca smiled back. 'All part of the job.'

Walking down the corridor towards Sotiris's office, Francesca wondered what he wanted to see her about. She was scheduled for a half-day and she'd planned to hurry home and have a swim before lunch. Her parents had gone over to see some friends on the other side of the island so she would have the place to herself. She could have a lazy time down by the water, nip into the kitchen for some bread and cheese and maybe a few figs...

Sotiris called, 'Come in,' as soon as she knocked.

'I gave young Costas a thorough examination, when I was able to pin him down long enough, and I think he could be discharged fairly soon,' Francesca said as she sat down beside Sotiris's desk. 'He's raring to go. The wound has healed very well and everything else is in good working order.'

'We'll send him home tomorrow.' Sotiris picked up the phone and spoke briefly to the Sister on Paediatrics.

'Sister's going to organise that,' he said, as he put the phone down.

Francesca glanced at her watch. 'So what did you want to see me about?'

'How about lunch?'

'Lunch? You mean...?'

Sotiris smiled. 'Lunch as in food. Will you have lunch with me today?'

'Well, yes. I've got a half-day.'

'So have I.'

'Ah, what a coincidence!'

Sotiris grinned. 'Or a neat bit of organisation.'

'So where are we going to have lunch?' Francesca was feeling more than a little surprised.

'I thought as it was such a glorious day I would take you out in the boat. I've packed some food and we can have a barbecue at the family beach house.'

'Sounds great.' She hesitated. 'Will some of the family be there?'

'Probably not.'

'How about Alex?'

'He's at nursery school today.' Sotiris raised an eyebrow. 'Any more questions, Francesca?'

'I'm sorry. It's just that when you spring a surprise on me like this, I do like to know what I'm in for.'

'Look, if it's going to be a problem...'

'Sotiris, it's not a problem.'

How could she explain that she hadn't thought he would ever get around to asking her out like this. She was feeling shell-shocked...but in the nicest possible way.

She stood up. 'I'll get my things and meet you in the reception area.'

Sotiris walked across to meet her as she hurried down the corridor from the staff cloakroom.

He smiled, that slightly lopsided, almost shy smile that tore at her heartstrings. For a successful consultant in his late thirties he could look decidedly boyish when he was off duty. He was wearing old jeans that clung to his muscular, athletic legs. His dark eyes had a lazy, sensual, easygoing expression as he looked down at her.

'What's with the luggage, Francesca?' Sotiris asked, removing the backpack she was holding and hoisting it effortlessly onto his shoulder.

Francesca smiled. 'That's simply my emergency pack. I always keep swimwear, towels, shorts and a change of clothing here just in case I get asked out for a picnic lunch.'

Sotiris laughed. 'How many picnic lunches have you had so far?'

'Far too many to count! But you're the best offer I've had today.'

'Glad to hear it.'

Sotiris led the way out of the hospital to his car. Francesca tried not to notice the inquisitive glances from the staff as they strolled out together through Reception.

'This is nice,' Francesca said, leaning back against the side of the boat as Sotiris pulled away from the harbour. It was a well-equipped boat, small enough for one person to handle and yet big enough to hold a few people.

'I bought this last week…no, don't worry, I'm an experienced sailor,' Sotiris added quickly as he saw Francesca's anxious expression. 'We have a larger family boat but I wanted to have my own for the time that I'm here. It's good to be independent. My family are great, but I sometimes feel a bit…"stifled," I think, is the word. Having said that, I don't know what I would have done without them during the bad times.'

Francesca moved closer to the wheel so that she could hear what Sotiris was saying. He seemed so relaxed now, it was almost as if he'd forgotten she was there. This was the real man she'd glimpsed and had wanted to be with from the first moment she'd met him. A man who wasn't holding back, checking every word he said in case…in case what? What was he hiding?

'It must have been hard for you when you were left with a small baby to bring up by yourself,' she prompted.

Sotiris hesitated, shifting his weight from one foot to the other as his fingers tightened on the wheel.

'It wasn't easy,' he said. 'When Sophia died, I…I had mixed emotions if I'm honest. I was obviously distraught when they phoned me from the Maldives to say there'd been an accident and…'

He broke off in mid sentence.

'Look, Sotiris, you don't have to tell me if you don't want to.'

'Oh, but I do.'

They were rounding the coast from the harbour, heading south, hugging the coast. The force of the wind took Francesca's breath away. Even on a hot day like this it felt chilly on the water. She pulled a sweater from her backpack.

Sotiris changed tack and ploughed straight through the waves, taking them head on until they reached a calmer stretch.

'I want to tell you about Sophia,' Sotiris said, relaxing again, with just one hand on the wheel. 'Then you'll understand why I feel like I do about…well, career-women. I know you don't approve of my outlook but…'

'Ah, yes, career-women. Like me, you mean?'

Sotiris turned soulful eyes towards her. 'Unfortunately, yes.'

'Why unfortunately?' She was still acting the part she knew he expected.

'Because career-women shouldn't commit themselves to long-term relationships.'

'Well, obviously not. I never would.'

She shifted her position on the wooden bench seat, leaning over to dip her hand in the water as the boat rushed through the now gentle waves.

'I'm glad that's how you feel, Francesca. Sophia thought she could have her cake and eat it. Is that what you say in English?'

'Word perfect. So why do you say that Sophia…?'

'I'd better concentrate on this stretch of water here if we're going to get to the island in one piece. Sometimes it's hard to talk about Sophia.'

'That's understandable,' she said softly, forgetting for the moment that she was still pretending to be the hard-hearted, brittle career type.

'Hold the wheel steady while I tie up,' Sotiris said, cutting the engine.

They had successfully arrived at the shore of the tiny, picturesque island, having negotiated the rocky entrance to the bay with its high overhanging cliffs. Francesca could see a long sandy, beautifully secluded, tree-shaded beach. It looked like paradise and it was completely deserted and unspoiled. There was only one dwelling place in sight.

'That must be your family beach house.' Francesca was pointing over at a long stone building on the edge of the shore.

Sotiris leapt from the boat, holding the rope in one hand. Tying the rope to a sturdy stone structure set firmly into the jetty, he turned to look in the direction that Francesca was pointing.

'Yes, that's the family house. Many years ago, it belonged to a family of sponge fishers. Then it was completely deserted for years, lived in only by goats for most of the time. My father found out who owned it when we were small and bought it. Then, every time we came over here for the day, he used to set to work, renovating it. As soon as I was big enough, I joined my older brothers in humping stones around and fixing pipes for the primitive plumbing we installed. Come and have a look.'

He held out his hand towards her. As she took his

hand she thought how handsome he looked when he was animated about a project. Far more exciting than when he was discussing the sad times in his life. She still wanted to know what had actually happened to his wife, but for the moment she was content simply to enjoy being with him.

The house was securely locked, and the shutters on the windows had to be unbolted before the light flooded in. Francesca walked around, looking in each room. The ground floor had a huge kitchen and a barbecue area outside that led straight onto the shore. The living room was comfortable, simply furnished. No frills, a couple of seascapes.

Yes, it definitely had the air of a fisherman's cottage. She climbed carefully up the glorified wooden ladder that served as a staircase. Upstairs there were four rooms, four sets of bunk beds, two double beds and two or three single beds.

'I've lost count of the number of people you could sleep here,' she called down the stairs.

Sotiris was unloading the boat, bringing the provisions into the kitchen. He paused, one foot on the bottom rung of the ladder.

'We had amazing family parties here when I was a child. And it was so exciting when we were allowed to sleep here.'

Looking down from the top of the ladder, Francesca felt a pang of longing. Sotiris was holding onto the ladder, his foot poised on a rung. If he'd begun to climb up now, she wouldn't have wanted him simply to give her a tour of the bedrooms.

'I'll come down and give you a hand,' she said quickly.

'All the stuff's in the kitchen now.'

He was still holding the ladder when she reached the bottom. He held out his hand as she reached the floor. She took it. He held on, looking down at her with quizzical eyes.

'So you like my little hide away?'

Francesca could feel her legs going limp at the sound of his deep, gravelly, sexy voice. She knew she was asking for trouble coming here alone with Sotiris, feeling as she did about him. Had he any idea what he was doing to her, simply by being near?

Abruptly he let go of her hand. 'Go and sit out at the front of the house. I'll bring you a drink when I've got the barbecue going.'

'I'd like to help.'

'Later you can sort out the salad I've brought, but I need to get this thing lit first.'

His voice was gruff now, as if he'd lost interest in her, almost as if he was wishing he hadn't brought her. She went out through the door to the front of the house where there was a sitting area, chairs and a rough wooden table right on the beach.

Sotiris gathered up some kindling and lit the barbecue, piling on charcoal till there was a healthy glow. He knew it would take him much longer if Francesca was near him. She affected him so profoundly he found it hard to concentrate on anything. It was OK in hospital, because he was trained to be professional there, but in the big outside world he just didn't know how to handle his feelings—that rush of adrenalin he felt whenever he met her, the longing to take her in his arms, the useless fantasising that she would be the one woman who would transform his life. If anybody could have been described as the woman of his dreams, then Francesca…

'Are you ready for me to do the salad now?'

'Yes, yes, of course.' Sotiris moved quickly to the kitchen table and pulled out the salad box. 'It's all in there—tomatoes, peppers, cucumber, lettuce and there's olive oil, wine vinegar and herbs to make the dressing.'

'Fine.'

'I promised us a drink,' Sotiris said, uncorking a bottle of white wine. 'I've had it in the cool-bag.'

'That's lovely.' Francesca took the glass he was holding out.

'The food can take care of itself for a while. Let's go and sit in the sun with our drinks.'

She followed Sotiris and sat down at the rustic garden table. She'd changed into shorts and a thin, sleeveless top, over a bikini.

'There's time for a quick dip before lunch,' Sotiris said, putting his glass down on the table.

Francesca smiled. 'That would be great!'

She pulled off her shorts and top. Sotiris was even quicker than she was as he sprinted down the shore in black swimming trunks that moulded themselves to his lithe, virile body in all the right places. Once in the sea, Francesca forced herself to concentrate on her swimming. They were simply two medical colleagues enjoying a day off duty together. Nothing more. There could be nothing more…

Nothing more than a light flirtation?

Sotiris was swimming next to her. His strong muscular body was very close. She turned over onto her back to gaze up at the glorious blue sky.

'This has got to be one of the most wonderful places on earth,' she breathed, almost to herself.

'You're right. It's heavenly isn't it?'

Sotiris was even closer now. He, too, was lying on his back, one arm almost touching hers. The salt water of the sea was so buoyant out here. It was holding her up as if she were lying on a floating mattress, with Sotiris beside her. She turned her head. He had the most seductive smile on his face. Gently, very gently, he reached towards her...and then he kissed her.

The taste of his lips and the saltiness of the sea mixed with something else more disturbingly erotic. His tongue was touching hers. She closed her eyes to enjoy the sheer bliss of this wonderfully sensual experience.

The blissful moment caught her off balance and suddenly she felt herself dropping beneath the surface of the water. But Sotiris's strong arms were holding her, pulling her against him.

'It's OK, I've got you, Francesca.'

The warmth of his chest in contrast to the cool sea was comforting.

'I'll take you back to shore,' he told her gently.

'I'm OK now.'

Sotiris gave her a rakish smile. 'Just pretend you're helpless for once in your life. I'll hold you on my chest and swim on my back.'

Francesca laughed. 'You just want some lifesaving practice, don't you?'

'Something like that.'

As she lay on top of Sotiris, being pulled through the sea to the warm shallow water, she knew this was one heady experience she would never forget. Whatever else happened in their relationship, this was the moment when she knew without a doubt that she'd fallen for Sotiris, hook, line and sinker.

How on earth was she going to handle this impossible situation? A light-hearted relationship was all she'd planned, but how long could she keep up a façade of indifference whilst putting her real emotions on hold?

Sotiris pulled her against him as they reached the shore. 'Are you sure you're OK now, Francesca?'

'I'm fine.' She moved out of the circle of his arms, heading with determined strides up the shore. 'The barbecue smells good.'

Sotiris laughed. 'I left a chicken rotating on the spit. I hope you like well-cooked chicken.'

'I love it.'

As she watched Sotiris moving over to the barbecue area she would have liked to call after him, And I love you, too.

But she must never say that. Never let Sotiris know about these real feelings deep inside her that had turned her world upside down.

She drew in her breath, whilst slowly counting to ten. She would go and take a shower. That might calm her down.

She found that the little room on the ground floor looked surprisingly well equipped for a remote island bathroom. Surprisingly, water came out of the taps and gushed down from the shower. There were several fluffy towels to choose from when she'd finished. Pushing her damp hair behind her ears, she thought she'd better get a move on.

'I hope I haven't kept you waiting,' she said, arriving back at the barbecue area.

'Not at all,' Sotiris said easily.

He topped up her wineglass as she joined him, wearing shorts and top again. Turning over the king-size prawns he'd spread on the barbecue, he said, 'What do you think of our primitive plumbing?'

'Amazing! I had an excellent shower.'

'There's a fresh water spring nearby. We simply re-routed it into some pipes and rigged up a pump... Would you pass that plate for the prawns?'

Francesca held out the large plate, before taking it, laden with prawns, to the table. Returning to the kitchen she gathered up the bowl of salad, a couple of plates and some cutlery.

Sotiris was setting out fresh crusty bread, olives and chicken on the table when she returned.

'Lunch is served, madam,' he said, holding out her chair. 'I'll be back in a moment. I forgot to get the lemon for the prawns.'

She smiled as she watched Sotiris reaching up to one of the lemon trees near the shoreline. Back at the table he chopped the lemon in half.

'I wonder why everything always tastes so good when you eat outside?' Francesca said.

'Not only eating outside but having the right company,' Sotiris said gently. He raised his glass towards her. *'Sigiya!'*

'Sigiya!' She clinked her glass against his.

It wasn't going to be easy to resist Sotiris if he made advances towards her. But did she want to resist him? Why should she? Why not simply go with the flow and work out the implications later...much later...?

She could tell by the way Sotiris was looking at her that he was thinking on similar lines. Seize the day, live for the moment...

She put down her fork exactly at the same moment as Sotiris. They looked at each other. It was almost as if they were telepathic. There was so much food still to be eaten but, temporarily, it didn't interest them. Sotiris stood up and took hold of her hands, pulling her to her feet.

She moved willingly into his arms. He bent his head and kissed her, oh so slowly, so maddeningly, enticingly provocatively, arousing her senses to a state of sensual excitement that needed more, much more than a mere kiss.

The expression in his eyes was pure heaven! All the longing, the passionate desire that she herself was feeling was mirrored in those dark grey pools.

'Yes,' she breathed.

His mouth was now so close to hers again. 'What was the question?' he whispered teasingly.

'I'm still waiting to be asked,' she said softly, all the hunger of her need blatantly obvious in the huskiness of her voice.

He bent down and lifted her into his arms. Gently he carried her over to the shady area beneath the lemon trees. There was a rug and two pillows spread in the cool shade.

Francesca smiled up at him as he laid her down on the rug. 'Did you think this was going to happen?'

'Not when I asked you out here this morning. But as soon as we got here, as soon as I began to know the real Francesca beneath the brittle exterior…'

'Am I brittle?'

'Only when you pretend to be. Deep down you're warm, you're sensual, Francesca you're wonderful…'

He was holding her against him. She could feel her excitement mounting as his hands caressed her. Their clothes were tossed aside as they clung to each other. Francesca could feel a deep primaeval urge that cried out to be satisfied. His caressing hands were driving her wild with desire. She felt as if she were being flown somewhere up into the heavens as their bodies fused together in an orgasmic ecstasy....

'Oh, yes,' she cried, as she climaxed. 'Oh, Sotiris, Sotiris...'

She was weeping with happiness. Sotiris was holding her, still deeply inside her. It was the most magical moment of her life. She didn't want it to end...

But it hadn't ended. They made love, until the sun was beginning to sink down towards the sea...

Francesca opened her eyes. Everything around her seemed so unreal...and then she remembered.

'Sotiris, what about Alex?'

Sotiris stirred beside her and pulled her into his arms. 'What about Alex?'

'Don't you have to get home?'

'Arwen is collecting him from school. She's taking him to Rhodes, with her own children, to stay with another of our sisters for the night.'

'You didn't tell me that.'

He raised himself on one elbow. 'Would it have made any difference if I'd said that there was a possibility that we were going to make love all afternoon with the option of staying here all night as well?'

His voice was husky, the expression in his eyes still dangerously sexy, wonderfully desirably, openly, blatantly wanting to make love with her again.

'Sotiris, be serious. You would never have dared to say that, would you?'

'I might, if I'd thought you could be tempted. But this morning I never dreamed there was the remotest chance you would agree to such a wild proposition.

Anyway, it just sort of happened. The sun, the sea, being close to you...'

He was pulling her into his arms again.

'I might be tempted again,' she whispered...

CHAPTER FIVE

'I'VE always wanted to spend the night on a desert island,' Francesca said, as she pulled on her sweater.

They were still sitting outside, watching the glow of the fire they'd lit by the edge of the shore. The remains of the barbecue was packed away ready to be taken back in the morning.

'Breakfast will be a strange meal,' Sotiris said, tossing another piece of driftwood on the fire. 'Cold chicken, bread, cheese, coffee…'

'Sounds good to me.'

The bright moonlight was illuminating the whole of the bay, shining silvery white on the surface of the water. Francesca could hear no sound except for the lap of the sea on the shore.

She took a sip from her mug of coffee. After their idyllic afternoon of love-making, they'd spent a short while trying to be practical, clearing up and preparing supper. Sotiris had found some potatoes and onions left behind from the last barbecue at the house and turned them into a delicious soup. Then they'd simply eaten some more of the prawns, chicken and salad left over from the lunch that had been abandoned in favour of spending a heavenly afternoon in the lemon grove.

Francesca phoned her mother on her mobile. 'Hi Mum, I won't be back tonight… No, I'm not at the hospital. I'm out enjoying myself… Don't worry. I can take care of myself… Yes, I love you, too…'

Sotiris was watching her. 'Your mother seems very understanding.'

'Of course she's understanding. She trusts me and she's always been very supportive. I've lived away from home for years. Made all the mistakes I'm ever going to make, I can tell you. Been through the fire, but it won't happen again.'

Sotiris stretched out on the rug by the fire, raising himself on one elbow. 'Do you want to tell me about it?'

Francesca tucked a cushion behind her head as she lay back, looking up at the stars. As she watched, one of them shot across the sky in a magnificent arc. Should she make a wish? Did she believe wishes came true? Could that star magic away her problems and make it possible for her to live like this with Sotiris for ever?

She closed her eyes. She wouldn't ask for the impossible.

'Francesca, if you don't want to tell me about…'

She opened her eyes. 'How long have you got?'

Sotiris smiled. 'All night, with nothing else to do but…'

He was leaning forward, his eyes going all misty again. She felt a shiver of renewed desire deep down inside her. Before she knew it they would be locked in each other's arms. Later…they must save their lovemaking till later because she wanted to have a coherent conversation with Sotiris. And above all, she wanted him to know where she was coming from.

'I started going out with a man called Jason. He was a partner in his father's firm in London. I was attracted to him when we met at the theatre one night. He had this expensive apartment overlooking the river, which was different from my one-bedroom flat in a high-rise block. Jason was fun to be with when I came off duty. It was like entering a different world, going out with him to films and the theatre—' She broke off. 'Listen. Is that an owl?'

Sotiris nodded. 'He's up in that tree. We mustn't disturb him. When we were kids we used to go to sleep listening to that weird sound. One of my brothers told me the hooting sound was a ghost when I was small. I was too scared to go to sleep so my dad had to bring me out here to show me that it was only a friendly bird.'

'You had a great childhood, didn't you?'

Sotiris smiled. 'So did you, I think. Like me, the problems came when you grew up. Tell me more about Jason.'

Reluctantly, she focussed her mind on the past again. 'He asked me to move in with him. We were happy for about six months and then he said he wanted to marry me and have children, so…'

Again she paused as she tried to work out how she was going to explain her reluctance to accept Jason's proposal.

'So why didn't you marry Jason? Was your career so important that you couldn't have put it on hold for a while?'

Sotiris's voice was solemn, with a sharp edge. She turned away so that he couldn't see the tears that threatened to spill out. Quickly, she stood up and moved towards the edge of the sea. Sotiris was walking quickly after her. He caught up with her and pulled her into his arms.

'What's the matter, Francesca?'

'Please, don't spoil everything by being judgemental, Sotiris. I can't help…I can't help the way I am. If I could change…if only I could change…'

He held her against him. 'I understand.'

She remained still, locked in his arms. He didn't understand. How could he? But that was all she was going to say about why she'd turned Jason down.

She raised her head and saw the tenderness in his eyes. 'Thanks for being so understanding. I can tell you what happened after I turned down Jason's proposal now. Let's go back to the fire. It's chilly down here by the sea.'

She curled up once more on the rug, watching the flames flickering. Sotiris beside her, was waiting for her to continue her story.

Francesca took a deep breath as the awful memories flooded back. 'I moved out, telling Jason I wasn't the girl for him.'

'Was he upset?'

Francesca gave a wry smile. 'Not for long. Within two months he'd transferred his affections and his new girlfriend was pregnant. They got married shortly afterwards. When the baby was two months old, Jason turned up at my flat one day, saying he'd made a terrible mistake. Marriage and children weren't as he'd imagined in his carefree bachelor days. His wife wanted to divorce him. She'd called him a hopeless father…'

She spread her hands wide in the flickering light of the fire. 'Oh, it was a long, long sob story. Jason was in tears as he begged me to come back to him. He said he wouldn't ask for marriage or children. He just wanted to be with me.'

'So what did you…?'

She swallowed hard as she remembered how difficult

it had been. 'I told Jason he must go back to his wife. I realised I'd had a lucky escape. I hadn't known what a hopeless, spoiled, selfish man he really was. And I was worried about his poor wife and the baby. I managed to get rid of him that evening, but he kept on pestering me, phoning me at all hours of the day and night, turning up at the flat when I was off duty. He said his wife had gone back to her parents. The divorce was going through. He simply didn't understand that I now loathed him. Once he even came to the hospital and made an awful scene.'

'That must have been wretched for you.'

'It was one of the lowest points of my life. I knew I had to do something. Jason wasn't going to go away, so I would.'

Sotiris leaned forward. 'I'm glad you came to Ceres.'

She looked at his handsome face illuminated by the fire and the moonlight.

'And I'm glad you came here as well. What made you want to leave Athens? Couldn't you have had Alex living with you in Athens?'

Sotiris gave a deep sigh. 'When Alex was born in Athens, my wife Sophia had no interest in him. She was an excellent surgeon and didn't want any interruption to her promising career.'

The owl's cry became louder. Sotiris leaned back, looking up at the darkening sky as he tried not to let the awful memories disturb the wonderful cosy ambience of being with Francesca beside the fire.

'I remember Sophia had suffered a chest infection and the antibiotics must have negated the effect of the Pill. When she first found out she was pregnant, she said she was going to have a termination. I begged her not to. She said, OK, she would have the baby but I would have to make all the arrangements to have the baby cared for and...' Sotiris broke off, standing up to move aside the dying embers of the fire with a thick wooden stick. 'It's time we went inside. It's getting chilly out here.'

He took Francesca's hand. She walked into the house with him, hoping he wouldn't lose the thread of his story.

'So, what arrangements did you make for the baby...for Alex?' she asked as they sat down on the ancient sofa in the living room.

'I employed a full-time nanny. Fortunately, she was excellent. Efficient, intelligent, and above all she loved little Alex. Not as much as I did...' He smiled, leaning his head back on a cushion. 'I loved him to bits. I used to rush home at every opportunity...'

'I can see why you would want to do that,' Francesca said softly. 'He's a wonderful little boy.'

She saw the look of surprise in Sotiris's eyes. 'I don't think you can begin to understand what it's like to have your own child. He wasn't just a patient, Francesca. He was my own flesh and blood.'

She swallowed hard. 'So why didn't you keep him with you in Athens?'

'When Alex was four weeks old, Sophia said she needed a holiday. She needed a complete break. She needed some exercise to get her figure back. Two weeks in the Maldives, diving. She was an expert scuba diver.'

'Sophia seems to have been an expert at everything.'

'Everything except being a wife and mother.' He paused. 'Two days after she arrived in the Maldives she was killed. Diving accidents can occur even to experts.'

'That must have been terrible for you. So, then you were left to bring up Alex by yourself.'

'When Alex was three months old, I brought him over to Ceres to be christened in the church where we'd all been christened—the church where my parents were married. It's up there on the hill.'

Sotiris waved his hand towards the dark hillside at the back of the beach house.

Francesca nodded. 'I remember seeing it from the sea as we arrived. Family means a lot to you, doesn't it?'

'I love my family very much. We're all very close. I have three brothers and three sisters. I'm the youngest. Everybody was worried about me having to bring up a baby by myself and continue with my demanding work as a consultant surgeon. I tried to reassure them that I had an excellent nanny, but they weren't convinced. My mother and sisters in particular begged me to leave baby Alex with them.'

'And so you became a part-time father.'

'That was what it felt like. I thought long and hard about it, but in the end I realised that Alex would benefit from having a loving extended family around him. And Arwen was so happy to have another baby in the house. Her children, Lefteris and Natasha, were no longer babies and she was hoping for another baby. She still is but it hasn't happened yet, unfortunately. There's still time, but meanwhile, Alex is very much her baby.'

'Didn't Arwen become possessive about Alex when she was caring for him all the time?'

'I'm afraid she did. My sister means well. She only has Alex's interests at heart. I made sure I got over here to Ceres to see Alex as often as I could. But that wasn't enough for me. Alex was happy enough, but I wanted to be more than a part-time father. I want to be with him all the time now.'

'If Alex were my son, I wouldn't want to leave him,' Francesca said quietly.

'I wouldn't have thought you would have understood how I feel,' Sotiris said huskily. 'But I really think you do.'

'I can imagine,' Francesca said quickly. 'So, remind me how you got this post at the hospital?'

'Michaelis came to Athens for a conference last year. I told him I wanted to spend more time on Ceres, so if ever the opportunity arose for a temporary post I'd like to take it. When he phoned me to ask if I'd like to take over from him for three months I jumped at the chance.'

'And after that, what will you do, Sotiris? You haven't resigned from your consultancy in Athens, have you?'

'No, I haven't resigned, Francesca. But...well, the way I'm feeling at the moment, I'd like to stay here for ever. What are you planning to do at the end of the summer?'

Francesca drew in her breath. 'I don't know. I don't think I'll ever be able to go back to London again. Not after living here on Ceres and...well, that's why I went off on my travels, wasn't it? To decide what I want from life.'

Sotiris's eyes narrowed. 'I thought you wanted a successful career, Francesca.'

She turned to face him. 'I'm beginning to see there's more to life than work.'

'I'm glad you think so.' He smiled. 'At this moment in time, I'd like to live here in this beach house, keep a few chickens, grow a few vegetables, teach Alex to read and write...' He broke off. 'Do you ever daydream like this, Francesca?'

'Oh yes. I can't think of anything more wonderful at this moment than a little house by the sea, a simple life and...' She stopped. She'd been going to talk about babies. Her taboo subject. 'I'd like a cat, a dog and maybe a donkey,' she said lightly.

Sotiris drew her against him. 'The reality is we're both on duty tomorrow morning, so we ought to get some sleep. That is, when we've said goodnight to each other, which might take a little while...'

When the first light of daybreak crept over the rustic window-sill Francesca opened her eyes to stare around her. At first she couldn't remember where she was. It wasn't like any bedroom she'd ever slept in. Wooden rafters overhead, wide open windows, the sound of the waves lapping on a nearby shore...

Sotiris, beside her, moved in his sleep and reality dawned upon her.

She tiptoed over the bare boards to the window. The view that met her was mind-blowing. The sea, coloured orange and red in the early dawn light, was as tranquil as a mill pond. Sotiris's boat shone in the warm rays of the sun, waiting to take them back to civilisation. On either side of the bay the tall cliffs stood sentinels to their secret hide-away. She felt as if this place was home. It had the most welcoming atmosphere. The walls seemed to wrap round her protectively.

'Come back to bed, it's too early to get up. We've got hours before we need to get to the hospital.'

Sotiris was holding out his arms towards her. She

went over to the bedside and knelt on the mat beside him.

'We ought to get a move on. There's lots to do and the journey back will take at least an hour.'

'Don't be so practical.' Sotiris leaned over and hauled her into bed. 'You feel so cold...'

By the time Francesca had allowed the warming-up process to begin she found her intentions of springing into action had blown out of the window. One heavenly hour later, she lay curled up in Sotiris's arms, wondering how ever she was going to make the transition to efficient doctor.

'We really should leave soon,' she whispered.

He held her tightly. 'Only if you'll promise to see me tonight. We'll go out for supper.'

'What about Alex?'

'Alex will be fine. He loves sleeping at Arwen's house in his old bedroom. He's got a new bedroom in our house but he enjoys being next door. Lefteris and Natasha spoil him, read him stories. They love pretending he's their little brother and—' Sotiris broke off. 'Hey, why are you looking so worried?'

'Was I looking worried? I'm not worried. I'm just thinking about how cosy it all seems to be part of that loving family. But don't you ever hope Alex will have brothers and sisters of his own?'

'Of course I do! But, that's all in the future. Meanwhile, Alex is happy, which is the main thing.'

Francesca turned away, setting her feet on the floor. She had to get back to reality. Stop wishing for the impossible. She'd been burying her head in the sand for long enough.

They walked into the hospital together. Sailing back over the water, Francesca had already decided that she wouldn't try to conceal her relationship with Sotiris from her medical colleagues and friends. They were both free to have a relationship. So long as it wasn't a permanent one. There must be no strings attached to this brief affair. Sotiris would have a future with someone else who could be a proper mother to Alex and have more babies. She herself would...well, she would just get on with the job in hand and make the most of her life.

As Sotiris had tied up in the harbour, she'd tried so hard to get rid of the feeling of belonging to him. The feeling that she was part of a couple. The reality was that they were both independent people free to live their own separate lives.

Sotiris put his hand on her arm as they walked down the corridor from reception. 'Would you like a coffee in my office?'

She smiled. 'No, thanks, I want to make a start. Got a busy day ahead.'

'I'll see you tonight.'

'Look forward to it.'

Francesca had successfully made the transition. She was on course again. As she always intended she would be after her romantic encounters with Sotiris. But, feeling the way she did about him, it wasn't going to be easy.

Her bleeper was going off already. Yes, she told Michelle in Reception, she would go to the emergency area immediately. She grabbed her stethoscope and put it around her neck.

Sister Eleni in Reception supplied her with a white coat.

'Would you examine the patient over there, Dr

Francesca?' Eleni said. 'The one who's screaming the place down.'

Francesca went over to the hysterical patient who'd just been brought in, strapped to a trolley. The young woman was throwing her arms around and kicking her legs.

Francesca took hold of the patient's hand while she spoke briefly to the worried husband of the disorientated woman.

'We're here on holiday, Doctor,' the distraught man said. 'My wife, Delphine, she's twenty-eight, she just went berserk this morning. She's been up all night, drinking water, and—'

'Drinking water?' Francesca queried.

'Oh, she's mad about water. Says she can't get enough of it. That's all she ever has. She hardly ever eats. She wanted to lose weight for this holiday, but I think she's lost too much, don't you, Doctor?'

'Yes, I do, but that's not the only problem.' Francesca looked down at her patient who had stopped screaming and was now clutching at Francesca's hand, staring up at her with wild eyes.

'How much weight have you lost, Delphine?' Francesca asked gently.

For a moment, a flicker of sanity returned as the patient focussed her eyes on the white-coated figure in front of her.

'I used to weigh thirteen stones. Now I'm about eight.'

'More like seven, and still going down,' her husband said.

He turned to Francesca. 'But the weight loss wouldn't make her go all hysterical, would it? She's been ranting and raving like a loony for the past three hours. We're supposed to fly back to England tomorrow, but I'd be scared to take her on the plane like this.'

'You'd better postpone your flight,' Francesca said quietly. 'I'm going to admit your wife. How much water has she drunk this morning?'

'I couldn't say, exactly. She never stops drinking the stuff. She buys bottles and bottles. Costs a damn sight more than my beer.'

'It's the water that's the problem,' Francesca said. 'I'm going to do a series of tests but I think we'll find that, by drinking all this water, your wife has reduced the sodium levels in her blood and caused a biochemical disturbance. In other words, she's suffering from acute water intoxication.'

'Blimey! I didn't know you could get drunk from drinking water!'

'Drinking anything to excess is dangerous,' Francesca said. 'It will take a while to sort out the imbalance in Delphine's body but we'll do all we can to ensure her recovery. It's a good thing you brought your wife in when you did.'

'Would it have been dangerous if we hadn't come in, Doctor?'

Francesca hesitated. 'It could have been fatal. Delphine is lucky to have a sensible husband like you. Once we've stabilised her, you must make sure she doesn't go down the same road again. You're going to need support when you get back to England, so we'll give you the medical case notes to take with you when we eventually discharge your wife.'

As Francesca was admitting her now sedated patient to the medical ward, Sotiris came through the door and walked up to the bedside.

'I heard there was a problem finding a bed on this ward, Francesca. I suggested to Sister that she should discharge one of her convalescent patients if she could find anyone suitable.'

Francesca smiled. 'Yes, it's all sorted. Sister's discharged a patient to carry on convalescing at home, with frequent outpatient visits. She's sitting in the patients' day room waiting for her family to collect her. But thank you for taking the trouble to check what was happening in person, Dr Sotiris.'

Sotiris smiled. 'I like to keep my finger on the pulse, Doctor.'

Turning to Delphine's husband, Francesca asked if he would like to stay at the hospital. He said that he would. Francesca said she would arrange it.

Sotiris was still waiting for her. She moved away from the bed and together they walked down the ward.

'I'm glad you've got everything sorted out with this case, Francesca.'

'I've sent blood samples to the path lab for analysis. Delphine's biochemistry will need careful monitoring. I think she'll have to be here for a week at least. But thanks for taking such an interest. It's not often I get preferential treatment from the medical director of the hospitals I work in.'

Sotiris smiled. 'I was concerned about this patient.' He lowered his voice. 'And when I heard you were taking care of her I was concerned for you. Are you OK, Francesca? Not too tired?'

She smiled back, feeling almost shy as she faced him. The past twenty-four hours had seemed like a lifetime, a lifetime of change. Nothing would ever be the same again and she had absolutely no idea how she was going to handle her disturbing feelings.

Where her newly admitted patient had a chemical imbalance, she herself had a complete emotional turbulence going on inside her.

'I'm fine.'

'It was good that you were able to make a quick diagnosis of this unusual case.'

'I remember treating a similar case in London. That patient was brought in too late to be saved. It was only in the post-mortem that the patient was found to be suffering from the biochemical disturbance, hyponatraemia, just like Delphine.'

'Well it looks as if you've started treatment early enough for Delphine.' Sotiris put his hand on her arm. 'Where are you off to now?'

'Paediatrics. I was on my way there when I was called to the emergency area. I always like to see Makis first thing in the morning.'

'Our little leukaemia patient.'

Francesca eyes clouded over. 'I expect the diagnosis will be confirmed soon. But until then...'

'You get very involved with your young patients, don't you, Francesca?'

She hesitated. 'Of course I do. Contrary to what you think, I love children. I'm very fond of Alex. I'd like to see him again soon. Next time we have a day off at the same time, would it be possible for the three of us to go out together?'

Sotiris took a step backward. 'I'm not sure that would be a good idea. Alex has to go to nursery school and—'

'Sotiris, he's only four. He could miss school for half

PLAY THE Lucky Key Game

and you can get

Do You Have the LUCKY KEY?

FREE BOOKS and a FREE GIFT!

Scratch the gold areas with a coin. Then check below to see the books and gift you can get!

▼ DETACH AND POST CARD TODAY! ▼

YES!
I have scratched off the gold areas. Please send me the **4 FREE BOOKS** and **GIFT** for which I qualify. I understand I am under no obligation to purchase any books, as explained on the back of this card. I am over 18 years of age.

M3GI

Mrs/Miss/Ms/Mr _____ Initials _____

BLOCK CAPITALS PLEASE

Surname _____

Address _____

_____

Postcode _____

🔑 🔑 🔑 🔑 4 free books plus a free gift   🔑 🔑 🔑 🔑 2 free books

🔑 🔑 🔑 🔑 4 free books   🔑 🔑 🔑 🔑 Try Again!

Visit us online at
www.millsandboon.co.uk

Offer valid in the U.K. only and is not available to current Reader Service subscribers to this series. Overseas and Eire please write for details. We reserve the right to refuse an application and applicants must be aged 18 years or over. Offer expires 31st December 2003. Terms and prices subject to change without notice. As a result of this application you may receive offers from Harlequin Mills & Boon and other carefully selected companies. If you do not wish to share in this opportunity, please write to the Data Manager at the address shown overleaf. Only one application per household.

The Reader Service™ — Here's how it works:

Accepting the free books places you under no obligation to buy anything. You may keep the books and gift and return the despatch note marked 'cancel'. If we do not hear from you, about a month later we'll send you 6 brand new books and invoice you just £2.60* each. That's the complete price - there is no extra charge for postage and packing. You may cancel at any time, otherwise every month we'll send you 6 more books, which you may either purchase or return to us - the choice is yours.

*Terms and prices subject to change without notice.

THE READER SERVICE™
FREE BOOK OFFER
FREEPOST CN81
CROYDON
CR9 3WZ

NO STAMP NEEDED!

If offer card is missing write to: The Reader Service, PO Box 236, Croydon, CR9 3RU

NO STAMP NECESSARY IF POSTED IN THE U.K. OR N.I.

a day...or we could take him out on a weekend. Alex and I got on so well when—'

'No, Francesca. I don't think I could arrange it.'

Francesca stared at Sotiris as she heard the finality of his tone. He'd never spoken to her like that before. Whatever his reasons, she wasn't going to pursue the subject, not at the risk of causing a rift between them. This was meant to be a brief fling for both of them and perhaps playing happy families would be going a step too far.

'Fine. It was just an idea, that's all.'

'No hard feelings?'

'Of course not.'

'So we're on for tonight?'

She smiled. 'Most certainly. See you later.'

She walked quickly away, not wanting Sotiris to see that she was upset. She'd hoped for a brief affair, and that was what they were now enjoying. But, oh, she knew she wanted so much more. She wanted with all her heart to start planning a future with Sotiris.

With Sotiris and little Alex. But that was impossible, as she had to keep reminding herself. She'd have to settle for what she'd got because there were only a few weeks left before Sotiris would return to Athens.

CHAPTER SIX

SAILING across from Nimborio Bay, Francesca leaned back against the side of the wooden seat, watching Manolis at the wheel. She felt as if she'd lived here on Ceres all her life. In the few weeks since she'd started work at the hospital she'd always enjoyed these early morning trips across the water.

What a way to start the day! Sun on her face, wind in her hair, cloudless blue sky...what more could she have wished for?

Only that life could go on for ever like this! The wonderful climate and friendly atmosphere of the people here on Ceres all contributed to her feeling of well being but the main source of happiness in her life now was her relationship with Sotiris. So long as she remembered not to look too far ahead, everything was sailing along wonderfully. Just like the Metcalfe family boat with Manolis at the helm was doing at the moment as it rounded the point leading into Ceres harbour.

During the past few weeks, Sotiris had engineered that they spent most of their days off duty together. It hadn't gone unnoticed at the hospital, but that didn't worry Francesca. There was no professional reason why they shouldn't both be absent from the hospital at the same time. Sotiris always appointed a deputy when he wasn't there and Francesca made sure there were doctors to cover her patients.

'Will you need a lift home this evening, Francesca?'

Manolis asked, as he held the boat steady for her to alight onto the quayside.

Francesca smiled. 'No, thanks, Manolis. I've got a half-day off duty, so I'll make my own way home later this evening.'

'Have a nice day!'

'You too, Manolis.'

She'd become very fond of Manolis and Maria his wife since living at the Nimborio house full time. She'd known them for a few years now since they'd come to work at the house before Francesca's father had actually bought it.

Francesca headed straight for the children's' ward as soon as she got into hospital. She was surprised to find that Sotiris was already there.

'*Kali mera*, good morning, Dr Francesca,' Sotiris said, in professional mode, fully aware that medical staff and patients were watching them.

Francesca smiled. It was strange to see the transition from the ardent lover Sotiris had been only hours before. '*Kali mera*. You're in here early.'

'Sister asked me to come and have a word with Makis. He didn't want to eat his breakfast this morning and he didn't sleep very well last night.'

Francesca sat down on the edge of Makis's bed. Myeloid leukaemia had been confirmed by the tests she'd performed on Makis and she'd begun injecting the drug interferon alpha just under his skin. Some of the initial symptoms weren't so bad now, but in the long term she knew she was going to have to instigate more radical treatment.

'How are you feeling now, Makis?' she said, reaching for the little boy's hand. It felt much too cold.

'I'm OK,' he said, listlessly. 'Just not hungry. I'm a bit fed up with being in hospital.'

Francesca leaned forward and spoke quietly to Sotiris. 'I think the air-conditioning in here is too cold, Sotiris. Most of the children run around for part of the day, but Makis gets too tired and spends a lot of time in bed, resting. We're nearing the end of September so the weather is cooling down. Let's have the air-conditioning switched off in here and the windows wide open.'

'I'll see to it,' Sotiris said, 'You're the paediatrician here. I value your opinion highly. Anything to ease life for Makis is worth trying.'

Makis had been straining to hear what was being said and his keen young ears had picked up the thread.

'I'd like to run around, Francesca,' the little boy said quietly. 'When are you going to make me better?'

Francesca looked across the bed at Sotiris and saw her own anxiety mirrored in his eyes.

'We're doing the best we can at the moment,' Francesca said. 'Your mother is coming in this morning to have a talk with us, Makis. After we've seen her we might be able to—'

'I know what you're going to say. Mum's already told me that one of my brothers might be able to help me get better. How would that work?'

'Well, first of all we'd have to be sure that your brother was a suitable helper for you,' Sotiris said carefully. 'Then, if he was, we would take some blood cells from his bone marrow—that's something found in your bones—and transplant them into you.'

Makis's eyes widened in astonishment. 'Have we got marrows growing in our bones?'

Sotiris smiled. 'Not that kind of marrow. It's another

substance that's very precious and special to each one of us.'

'And would that stop me feeling tired?'

'It could certainly make you feel better than you do now,' Francesca said cautiously.

Even if one of the brothers proved to be a suitable donor for a bone-marrow transplant, there were so many complications that could arise. She didn't want to raise the little boy's hopes too much.

'But while we're sorting all that out, wouldn't you like to have another try at eating some breakfast?' Sotiris said gently. 'I've got a little boy called Alex who's only four, and he ate all his breakfast this morning.'

'What did Alex eat?' Makis asked, looking interested as he pulled himself up against the headboard at the back of his bed.

'Alex had honey from the bees on the hillside behind our house and—'

'I like honey.'

Francesca rearranged Makis's pillows, plumping them up to make him more comfortable.

'If I go to the kitchen and get some honey and a piece of nice fresh crusty bread, will you eat it, Makis?' she asked.

Makis smiled. 'OK. Will you tell me some more about Alex? Is he big for his age?'

'Quite big,' Sotiris said. 'He always finishes everything on his plate. But he's not as big as you yet.'

'I'm eight,' Makis said proudly. 'I'm going to work on the boats like my dad when I grow up…'

Francesca and Sotiris glanced at each other, both reading the other's anxious thoughts. *When I grow up…* The little boy's phrase was so poignant. They continued to chat easily with Makis, mostly about Alex. As soon as Francesca felt it was OK to leave their little patient, she said she was going to the kitchen.

Sotiris said goodbye to Makis and walked with Francesca to the end of the corridor that led to the kitchen.

'You don't have to do this yourself, Francesca,' he said, his eyes tender. 'You could send someone.'

Francesca smiled. 'I like waiting on Makis. And I want to be there in the ward to make sure he eats at least some of his bread and honey. I'll go around my other patients while I'm waiting, of course.'

Sotiris smiled back. 'You've got a warm heart Francesca. Look, I've got to be in Theatre in ten minutes so I must go. How do you feel about a walk when we go off duty this afternoon? We could take the boat down the coast somewhere and…'

'Sounds great. We could pick up some lunch from the shops on our way down to the harbour.'

'Good idea. See you later.'

Francesca spent the rest of the morning in the children's ward. She broke off to meet Makis's mother in Sister's office to explain what would be involved in a bone-marrow transplant. Makis's mother agreed that she would like to have her other children checked out for suitability as donors.

'Anything that can improve Makis's chance of a better life is a good move,' she said as she signed the form authorising Francesca to go ahead and make tests on her children.

Francesca met Sotiris at the end of the morning and together they walked out through the main door of the hospital.

'Sotiris! Sotiris!'

An elderly lady was hurrying up to the door, a little boy trotting along beside her.

'Francesca!' The little boy hurled himself at her.

Francesca smiled. 'Alex! What are you doing here?'

'We've come to see Daddy. Grandma says he's going to look after me this afternoon.'

'Sotiris, thank goodness I've caught you.' Alex's grandmother paused to catch her breath. 'I've had such a busy morning.'

'I thought Alex was with Arwen.'

'No, she had to go to a meeting at the school so I told her to bring Alex to me. Hello, I'm Irini, Sotiris's mother,' she said to Francesca, in perfect but charmingly accented English. 'Do you work here?'

Francesca smiled as she held out her hand. 'Yes. I'm Francesca Metcalfe.'

Irini Popadopoulos smiled back. 'I think I met your father and mother once at a dinner given by the mayor. Your father is a doctor, isn't he?'

Francesca was warming to this charming lady. Her appearance belied her age and the fact that she had seven children and heaven knew how many grandchildren. She could see where Sotiris got his charm and handsome good looks from.

'Yes, Francesca's father is a doctor and so is she. One of my most trusted colleagues,' Sotiris said.

'That's nice. I've got to go over to Rhodes to see my sister, Sotiris, so I've brought Alex for you. I'd forgotten I'd promised I'd meet my sister Kristina until she rang up a short time ago to remind me. I scribbled a note for Arwen to say that Alex is with you, Sotiris.

Then I got a taxi down the hill and if I'm quick I'll just catch the boat... Oh, I'm so out of breath!'

'I'll give you a lift to the boat,' Sotiris said, taking his mother's arm. 'Now you mustn't go rushing around like this. Slow down or—'

'Oh, I'm fine, Sotiris. Just because you're a doctor it doesn't mean you have to start worrying about me. I'm as fit as I ever was. Get a bit breathless now and again but who doesn't? Ooh, you'll have to help me up this big step. Why on earth you have to have a car that's so high up, I don't know... All these unnecessary cars clogging up the streets. When I was a girl we were lucky to catch a ride on a donkey...'

Sotiris hoisted his mother into the front seat. Francesca sat in the back with Alex. He grinned mischievously as he settled himself beside her.

'I keep asking Daddy when he will take me over to your house again, Francesca, but he is always too busy. I sometimes see Samantha and Rachel when they come to play with Natasha.'

'Yes, they told me they've seen you, Alex,' Francesca said, becoming aware that Sotiris was watching her in his rear-view mirror as he drove down to the harbour. He was frowning and his eyes were solemn and anxious.

The Rhodes ferry was about to depart. Sotiris screeched to a halt on the quayside and waved to one of the sailors who was about to draw up the boarding ramp. The sailor waved back in acknowledgement, his hand still on the iron chain, waiting patiently as Sotiris helped his mother down from the car.

'When are you coming back, Mum?' he called as his mother hurried on board.

'*Avrio.* Tomorrow.' A quick wave and she was off into the cabin.

'Goodbye, Grandma!' Alex waved to the departing ferry.

'Have you had lunch, Alex?' Francesca asked as they got back into the car.

The little boy shook his head. 'Grandma was making lunch when she got this phone call from my Great-Aunt Kristina, telling her not to forget she was going to meet her in Rhodes today. But she'd already forgotten—Grandma's always forgetting things—so we set off in a big rush but first I had to catch Joey.'

'Who's Joey?'

'He's Grandma's parrot. He lives in a cage but she lets him out when I go to see her and he flies all round the house.'

'When my brother Vasilios went to the States, he gave the parrot to my mother,' Sotiris explained as he waited on the harbourside to negotiate a gap between two lorries delivering goods to the shops. 'I think I'll park round that corner because we might be here a long time.'

As they all alighted from Sotiris's parked car, which he'd managed to squeeze in beside a skip full of stones and a small boat, Alex was still telling Francesca about the wonderful parrot.

'Alex obviously adores Joey,' Francesca said to Sotiris.

Sotiris groaned. 'He's always going round there to see him. My mother doesn't seem to mind how many of her grandchildren troop in and out of the house but I think she should be able to have some rest during the day. My brother's a teacher and last year he took his young family and went to work in America.'

Francesca smiled. 'So Grandma got the parrot.'

Sotiris nodded. 'Vasilios's house was empty for a few months and then when I decided to come here for three months it was convenient to move into Constantinos Street alongside the rest of the family.'

'I like living near Grandma and Joey,' Alex said, holding hands in between Francesca and Sotiris. 'Can we have something to eat now? I'm starving.'

Francesca smiled. 'In that case, we'd better go and buy something. Would you like to come on a picnic with Daddy and me?'

'Ooh, yes, please.'

'Francesca,' Sotiris said, quietly, 'I think it might be best if I look after Alex by myself. You've been taking care of children all morning and it's your off-duty time now, so—'

'No!' Both Francesca and Alex spoke together, after which they looked at each other and smiled in agreement.

'I'd like to spend the afternoon with you and Alex,' Francesca said.

'And I want Francesca to be with us, Daddy.'

Sotiris gave a deep sigh. 'In that case, I suppose I'm outnumbered.'

'Yes!' Alex punched the air as he'd seen his big cousin Lefteris do after he'd scored a goal when he was playing football. 'Can we take the picnic down to the beach house?'

Francesca looked at Sotiris. The house had become very special to them over the last few weeks.

'Why not?' Sotiris said, in a resigned tone.

Francesca smiled, holding tightly to Alex's hand as he skipped along beside her into the bakery. Glancing at Sotiris, she saw that he'd come to terms with whatever was worrying him. Or was his expression one of accepting the inevitable? Over the past few weeks she'd realised that he had a genuine aversion to her mixing with his family.

So the beach house had become their secret hideaway. There was also Sara's house which had proved to be a godsend. But why was Sotiris so reluctant to let her mix with his own family? It wasn't as if...

'Dad wants to know whether you want some of those lamb pastry things. Kleftiko we call them. Grandma makes them with cheese, onion and lamb and I like them a lot.'

Francesca looked across at Sotiris who was standing by the counter in a shop, patiently waiting for her answer.

'You all right, Francesca?' he asked softly.

'I'm fine! Sorry, I was miles away. Yes, please, I love kleftiko and perhaps some spanakopita, a little of that delicious-looking taramasalata, a few olives and...'

She moved forward to take an interest in what was going on inside this fascinating shop.

'I'm still starving,' Alex said, as he leapt ashore and ran towards the beach house.

'Lunch coming up!' Sotiris said, hauling the large box of food from the boat onto the shore.

'I already gave Alex some bread and cheese while we were on the boat,' Francesca said, lifting the bag of salad as she followed Sotiris up to the house.

'He's got hollow legs,' Sotiris said. 'OK, Alex, hold on a minute till I find the key. There you are. Now you can...'

Alex had disappeared up the ladder, shouting with delight to be back. 'Haven't been here for ages.'

Francesca was feeling guilty as she looked at Sotiris. 'We could have brought Alex with us sometimes.'

The anxious expression returned. 'No, we couldn't. We shouldn't have brought him here today.'

Francesca took a deep breath. 'Well, whatever reasons you have, let's just enjoy our time with Alex today. He's a wonderful little boy. I love him. I really do…'

'Don't, Francesca!' Sotiris pulled her against him. 'Please, I can't explain but…yes, you're right about today. Let's just enjoy it. Let's pretend…well, we'll just imagine it's a special sort of day.'

He smiled down at her and gently touched her lips with his own. Francesca clung to him, feeling relieved that he'd stopped frowning. This was the Sotiris she was in love with. He hadn't changed. He still seemed to love her as much as she loved him.

His kiss deepened. 'Oh, Francesca,' he whispered, huskily. 'If only…'

They could hear Alex climbing back down the ladder. Sotiris pulled away.

'Lunch, Alex!' he called. 'Come and help me set the chairs around the table by the shore. Where would you like to sit?'

'Here, next to Francesca.'

'I thought you might,' Sotiris said.

It was a free and easy picnic. Francesca brought some plates and glasses from the kitchen and Sotiris opened the bottle of wine and a carton of apple juice.

'I'm full now,' Alex said, patting his stomach to prove the point. 'Can I go in the sea, Daddy?'

'You can go in the sea but don't swim yet. It's too soon after lunch. When it's OK to swim, Francesca and I will swim with you.'

'Whee!' Alex was running down to the edge of the water, stripping off his shorts and T-shirt, dropping them on the shore as he went into the water.

Soon he was sitting down in it, splashing his little hands, while he sang a Greek song that he'd learned at nursery school. Francesca watched him fondly. She loved this little boy, in a different way to his father but with the same intensity. She could hear the words of the song clearly now it was being sung for the third or fourth time. Something about a sailor and a boat.

She got up from the table and lay back on the rug that Sotiris had spread on the edge of the shore. He joined her and both of them kept a careful watch on Alex playing in the water.

'Alex has such a lovely voice,' Francesca said. 'And I can understand what he's singing about because his Greek is very distinct. The song is so typical of this island. This wonderful island, sea, sun, ships... Oh, I'd like to be able to live here for ever...'

'You could if...' Sotiris hesitated as he put an arm around her shoulders, drawing her closer to him. 'If you were to change your ideas about wanting a career. In the few weeks I've known you I've come to realise that deep down you're not the kind of woman you'd like everybody to believe you are. You're a much warmer, kinder person. You love children and...'

He broke off, searching for the right words. He was sure he could express his feelings in Greek but he was afraid it wouldn't sound the same in English.

Francesca could feel herself melting as his hand closed around hers. 'Yes, I love children,' she said. 'But I could never be a mother.'

'But you could! It's possible to have a career and children as well. If both mother and father pull together towards the same ends, it would work. Can't you see that?'

'Oh, Sotiris!' For a moment she clung to him, before pulling away and rising to her feet. 'It's not what you think. You think I've got a choice, don't you? Well I haven't. I—'

'Francesca, come and look at this fish!' Alex called.

'Why haven't you got a choice? Tell me, Francesca...'

Francesca pulled a tissue from the pocket of her shorts and wiped her damp cheeks as she ran towards the water. Sotiris followed. When she turned to look at him she saw that his eyes were deeply troubled.

'I've said more than I meant to. Just forget what I said, Sotiris.'

'No! You must explain.'

She gave a heavy sigh of resignation. 'It won't make any difference. It's something I've learned to live with and I don't want you to become involved.'

'It's swimming away now, Francesca,' Alex called. 'Look it's over there now! It liked me. It was talking to me. It said...'

Alex made a face like a fish and imitated the way the fish had moved its mouth.

'Oh, Alex!' Francesca caught hold of the little boy. 'You're adorable!'

Sotiris came up behind her as she sat down beside Alex in the shallow water, ignoring the fact that her shorts were now soaked.

'You can't be sad for long when you've got a child around you,' Francesca said quietly.

'Francesca we've got to talk,' Sotiris said. 'What did you mean when you said—?'

'Not now, Sotiris. Later perhaps...I don't know.'

She was confused. She'd said too much already. But she loved Sotiris so much she owed him an explanation. She'd never meant it to go this far when she'd embarked on a light-hearted relationship. She'd never meant to become totally involved with him and his family.

'I'll hold you to that,' he said quietly. 'We can't go on like this.'

Alex had waded away and was walking towards deeper water. Sotiris moved quickly.

'Alex, hold my hand. We'll have a swim soon.'

The rest of the afternoon was spent in the water or on the shore, stretched out on towels. After Francesca had changed into her bikini she hung her shorts out to dry on the washing line near the kitchen door before joining Alex and Sotiris in the sea. Her shorts would be stiff with the sea water but she didn't care. This was a special day. Probably the last day she would spend with Sotiris and Alex. Because when she explained the full extent of her medical problems, that would put an end to any thought Sotiris might be harbouring of a future with her.

They swam in the shallow water, the three of them close together, with Alex in the middle. The little boy shouted and laughed, swallowing water but still working hard at improving his strokes.

'I'm a fish! I'm a big fish. Watch me dive, Francesca!'

Francesca watched anxiously as Alex dived down, then surfaced several metres away from them.

'He's OK,' Sotiris said, putting a hand on her shoulder. 'No need to look so worried. He's been swimming since he could walk. I used to bring him here, sometimes just the two of us, sometimes with his cousins.'

'Sounds wonderful!' Francesca said, breathing deeply to keep herself from feeling sad.

The thought that all this would have to end was almost too much to bear. But she would remember this day. She would remember every precious moment.

'I'm a big fish, coming to get you, Alex,' she called as she swam towards him.

'No big fish!' Alex cried, joining in the game. 'I'm the big fish now and I'll chase you… Grr…'

'That's not a fish, that's a lion, Alex.' Sotiris laughed.

'OK, I'm a lion, a sea lion. Grr, grr… Now I'm a dolphin. Dolphins are nice. We had a dolphin here in the bay, didn't we, Daddy?'

Sotiris was treading water now, staying close to his son, one hand lightly touching Francesca's arm.

'Yes, we did. A baby dolphin who was looking for his mummy.'

'Did he find her?' Francesca asked.

'Yes, but we had to help him,' Alex said excitedly. 'I swam one side of him and Daddy swam the other until he went back to the sea where his mummy was waiting.'

Francesca was committing this tender moment to her memory as she lay on her back, eyes closed against the bright glare of the sun's rays, feeling the lapping of the water against her and the touch of Sotiris's hand giving her the same sensation she had when he was caressing her before they made love.

'We should be getting back,' Sotiris said regretfully.

'Not yet,' Alex pleaded. 'Let's stay here all night. Why can't we, Daddy?'

'Well, for one thing, Arwen might wonder where

we were. I don't know what Grandma put in her note and—'

'You could phone and find out, Daddy.'

'No, we really must go,' Sotiris said, reaching out to his son.

'OK. I'll race you back to the shore. I can beat both of you…'

The three of them landed on the shore, laughing and spluttering after the improvised race. Sotiris and Francesca had deliberately held back towards the end so that Alex could emerge triumphant.

'I won! I won!'

Sotiris picked up his son, slung him over his shoulder in a fireman's lift and ran up to the house.

Francesca followed them but more slowly. She was in no hurry for this day to end. It might be the last time she ever saw the beach house again. At least with Sotiris here. In years to come when she returned to Ceres for a nostalgic visit she might just be strong enough to take a boat round into this bay and look at the place where she'd enjoyed the happiest moments of her life.

They were drawing near to Ceres harbour. Alex, who'd been snoozing in Francesca's arms for the last half-hour, suddenly opened his eyes.

'Where are we?' Alex asked.

'Nearly home,' Sotiris said, steering the boat towards the quayside. Francesca put Alex on the seat beside her before standing up and uncoiling the landing rope. They were almost on the quayside. She'd tied up before a few times when she'd come out in the boat with Sotiris.

Sotiris was holding the boat steady. Francesca leapt onto the quayside and began tying up.

'Hello, Francesca!' Natasha was standing beside her.

'Hello, Natasha,' Francesca said, surprised to see Alex's cousin. 'Is your mother with you?'

'Yes, I'm here.' A small, dark-haired lady was making her way over the rough cobblestones, her car keys swinging in her hand. 'I'm Arwen. We haven't met before.'

'I'm Francesca Metcalfe.' Francesca held out her hand.

Arwen's eyes held a hostile expression and she didn't take hold of the outstretched hand. 'I know who you are.'

Arwen's harsh tone was totally unexpected. Francesca stared at the woman in front of her. Could this really be Sotiris's sister, Natasha's mother? The woman who Chloe had said was so hospitable and helpful, always offering help with the twins, inviting them to her house, picking them up from school...

'Go and wait in the car, Natasha,' Arwen said evenly. 'And take Alex with you.'

'Alex, come and get in the car,' Natasha said, with the practised authority of a bigger child as she reached for her small cousin's hand.

'Is Lefteris there?' Alex asked.

'Yes, he's got a new football. He's having a football party with some of his friends from school and you're invited.' Natasha said, taking hold of Alex's hand.

Alex pulled himself to his full four-year-old height. 'Great!'

He trotted along happily beside his cousin. Suddenly he turned and waved his hand. 'Are you coming up home, Francesca?'

Francesca smiled nervously. 'I can't come today, Alex.'

'Or any day,' Arwen said quietly in Greek.

Sotiris had now joined the group on the quayside. Arwen rounded on him, speaking in rapid Greek. 'Sotiris, you promised me you wouldn't let Alex get involved with this woman.'

'Now, just a minute, Arwen…' Sotiris began angrily.

Francesca steeled herself. The exchange between brother and sister that followed was heated, but she gathered what was being said. Apparently, Arwen had been told that she was a career-woman, with no interest in ever having children. Arwen had insisted that it would be ruinous to have a liaison with someone whom Alex might come to regard as a mother figure.

'What about when she tires of her relationship with you, Sotiris? What about when it's all over and little Alex wants to see her again? He's already grown fond of her. I could see that when he spoke just now. Sotiris, whatever were you thinking about to take that woman to the beach house, the family beach house where—'

'That's enough!' Sotiris said, in clear, firm English. 'How dare you speak about Francesca like that? Francesca is the woman I love and I won't have you discussing her in that rude manner. Francesca understood everything you said just now and—'

'Yes, I understood,' Francesca said. 'And I can see that Arwen has a point, Sotiris. I believe that your sister only has Alex's interests at heart. We all have. Alex has to be our priority. He mustn't get hurt.'

For a few moments, Arwen looked stunned by Francesca's unexpected reaction.

'I have to go,' Arwen said quickly. 'I need to get the children home. Spiros will wonder where I've got to. We're having a football party in the field at the back of the house and Lefteris's friends will be arriving soon. I'll put Alex to bed at our house afterwards, Sotiris. All the other boys are staying and he would feel left out if he had to go home.'

'Thank you. We'll talk tomorrow.'

'I think we'd better.' Arwen turned and walked away, without a backward glance at Francesca.

'She means well, Sotiris,' Francesca said. 'She's a good, kind-hearted woman.'

'Yes, she is. So are you to take it so well. I'll talk to her tomorrow, but I'd like you and me to have a long talk tonight.'

Francesca looked uncertain. 'We need to clear the air. I haven't been totally frank with you. I've been holding back and now I think I need to be more open. Let's go to Sara's house.'

CHAPTER SEVEN

FRANCESCA was glad that Sara and Michaelis had installed security lights in their house before they'd gone off on honeymoon. She could see the glow of the lights now from the top of the hill as Sotiris drove down the narrow road. Whenever she was there she made sure that the place looked lived in from the outside. It was a large, impressive house, in a completely isolated setting, and Francesca took her responsibilities seriously.

Although she'd heard that crime on the island was almost non-existent, she knew it was best to be safe. The inhabitants of Ceres were totally honest but there could be the odd rogue tourist who might decide to break into an empty house that looked as if it had rich pickings. It was unlikely, given the type of person attracted to this part of the world, but not to be ruled out.

Francesca put her key in the door and went inside, Sotiris following as she began to make her way to the kitchen.

'I stocked up on food and wine when I was here a few days ago, so I'll make us some supper before—'

'No.' Sotiris gently spun her around and drew her towards him. 'We have to talk before we do anything else. Go on to the terrace, Francesca, and I'll bring drinks out there.'

Francesca looked up into his eyes. His expression was tender but troubled. She had to put him out of his misery. At least, knowing how futile a permanent relationship would be, he would see why their relationship had reached the point where it couldn't go any further.

She went out through the long plate-glass windows onto the rather grand crazy-paved area with views over the valley. Far below, she could see the bay, with lights from the moored boats twinkling on the dark water.

Sitting down on the small wicker sofa, she leaned back against the squashy feather cushions. It was so nice to have a place where she felt completely at home. Sara had insisted she regard it as her own home, and she certainly did! She always made sure now that there was wine, fruit and vegetables in the fridge. On the days when she was planning that she and Sotiris might have a meal here, she would bring in a chicken, some fish or a Greek delicacy from one of the shops in the village.

Sotiris came out to the terrace with a bottle of wine, glasses and a bowl of olives on a tray which he set down on the table beside the wicker sofa. Handing Francesca a glass he sat down next to her.

'*Sigya!*' He raised his glass and clinked it against hers.

She returned the toast before taking a sip and then a larger gulp from her glass as she realised that Sotiris was waiting for her to begin her explanation.

'Take your time,' he said gently. 'But I want to hear everything.'

She took a deep breath. 'I'm sterile,' she said quietly. 'I can't have children.'

Sotiris set his glass down on the table and leaned forward to cradle her in his arms.

'Oh, my poor darling. I had no idea. Why didn't you tell me before?'

'I find it hard to admit even to myself. When the consultant told me I would never have children I just tried to stop wanting them, but I never succeeded…'

It was as if the floodgates had opened on all her misery. She wept, while Sotiris held her in his arms, rocking her as if she were a baby. Suddenly, she knew she had to come to her senses again. Sotiris would want to know more.

Gently, she drew back from him until she was leaning against the arm of the sofa. Sotiris handed her a large white handkerchief.

'Thanks.' She dabbed her eyes. 'I've never cried like that before about…about my problem. Not even when the consultant first told me. My mother cried but I didn't.'

'When…when did you find out that you couldn't have children?'

'I was sixteen. I'd gone off on a camping holiday in Devon with school at the end of the summer term. I hadn't felt well for the first few days but I thought it was a change in diet or something so I didn't mention it to any of the teachers. In the middle of the night I woke up with the most awful stabbing pain here.'

She put her hand low down on the right side of her body.

Sotiris leaned forward, concern in his eyes. 'The pain was in the right iliac fossa?'

'Yes, I had appendicitis. Being a doctor's daughter and studying biology in the sixth form, I thought it might be. I managed to get out of the tent in one of the times when the pain had subsided somewhat. I remember making my way to the caravan where my class teacher was sleeping. By the time I'd managed to rouse her she wasn't too pleased to see me in the middle of the night.'

'But surely she got you off to hospital, didn't she?'

Francesca sighed as the memories flooded back. 'Sotiris, with the benefit of hindsight it's easy to see what should have been done but, remember, I was only sixteen and completely in awe of anybody in authority. When my teacher told me it was probably something I'd eaten and I would feel better in the morning, I had no alternative but to go back to my tent and sweat it out.'

'Didn't she take your temperature?'

Francesca shook her head. 'Look, Sotiris, I've long since forgiven her for being so unsympathetic. She was young herself and she didn't realise how serious it was. Anyway, as the pain grew more and more excruciating I just got on with it. I think at one point I blacked out for a short time, which was a merciful release from the pain. I've never been so pleased to see the sun coming up. By this time I was beside myself. I started to scream so that somebody would come to me... somebody...anybody...'

Sotiris covered her hand with his own. She gripped it as she relived the pain.

'One of the men teachers came running into my tent and said something like, "Oh, my God!"

'I remember he picked me up and carried me over to one of the staff caravans and then it's all a blur. An ambulance came...then I was in hospital...they were operating...when I was fully round my parents were there. They stayed with me for days. My appendix had burst and there was a generalised infection of the abdominal cavity.'

'Peritonitis. Very dangerous. Oh, you poor lamb.' Sotiris stroked her hair.

'My father had me transferred to the hospital where he was working and one of his colleagues, James Morton, who was a close friend of ours—he'd known me since I was a baby—took over my case. I was in hospital weeks and weeks while they tried to get rid of the peritonitis.

'Then they did scans and tests to find out how much damage had been done. That was when James broke the news that there had been extensive scarring in the abdomen, which had affected my Fallopian tubes. They were completely blocked. I should resign myself to not having children.'

'But didn't James Morton suggest you could have surgery to unblock your fallopian tubes?'

'No. I was sixteen years old, glad to be alive after all I'd been through. If he'd suggested more treatment I would have said no. I couldn't take any more.'

'Not then, but in the future! Surely...'

'No, Sotiris, his advice was that it was better to get used to the idea of being childless. Tubal surgery is a very delicate operation and he said that with the amount of scarring involved my tubes wouldn't be viable anyway. He pointed out that I was planning a career in medicine, that I would get great satisfaction from my chosen profession. He suggested I sublimate my maternal instincts by becoming a paediatrician.'

'What did you say to your consultant friend?'

'You have to remember, I was only sixteen years old. I'd been working hard for my exams. I'd been looking forward to becoming a doctor from an early age. The full implication of being childless hadn't really sunk in. I put it to the back of my mind. I focussed on my career with even more determination when I knew that was all I had.'

'But you know as well as I do that tubal surgery is improving all the time. I know it's had a poor record of success in the past but—'

'Please, Sotiris, don't say any more. I made a decision to accept my sterility and I don't want to reconsider. My life has been very fulfilling and there's no reason why I should—'

'No reason? There's every reason! You would be the most perfect mother in the world. I've seen how Alex adores you, how your young patients in hospital can't get enough of you. Francesca, the decision you made at sixteen—'

'No, Sotiris.' Francesca leaned forward and placed her finger on his lips. 'Hush, please. Don't say any more because it won't change anything. I've come to terms with my life and for most of the time I'm happy and fulfilled.'

She swallowed hard. That wasn't true at the moment, but she didn't want Sotiris to become any more involved with her problems. Because she loved him so much she wanted to think that he would one day find someone who could be a good wife and mother to Alex and the children they would have together. The thought made her feel stronger.

'Sotiris, you mustn't become involved with my problems. You have your whole life in front of you,' she said carefully. 'When Michaelis returns in November, you'll be able to go back to Athens and resume your life there.'

'My life will never be the same again,' Sotiris said evenly. 'I love you, Francesca. The fact that you can't have children makes no difference to me. Please, Francesca, will you marry me?'

Francesca drew in her breath. Marriage to Sotiris would be the most wonderful joy in the world, but she couldn't accept it. It wouldn't be fair on Sotiris. Whatever he thought now, he might change in the future when the full implications kicked in.

'Sotiris, I can't marry you, knowing that I would be depriving you of the joys of a real family. I know how you love Alex. How he would love to have brothers and sisters of his own. I'm deeply honoured that you should ask me, but the answer has to be no.'

Her heart was breaking. Only moments ago she'd thought she was strong enough to bear the burden of her sterility and all it implied, but now she knew she was still vulnerable. Especially when the most wonderful man in the world had just asked her to marry him.

She could feel the tears threatening again. Sotiris's arms were already around her. 'Don't cry, my darling. Whether you marry me or not, I'm always going to be here for you…'

'No, Sotiris, we can't go on like this…'

Sotiris's lips on hers silenced her. Gently and, oh, so tenderly he picked her up in his arms and carried her through the terrace door back into the house.

'I want to make love to you,' he whispered, his voice husky as he carried her up the wide staircase. 'I've never wanted to be with you as much as I do at this moment.'

He carried her through into the guest room, the room which they'd come to regard as their own. Gently, he laid her down on the bed, his eyes scanning her face.

'You may as well know, I don't give up easily,' he

said, a tender smile on his sensual, sexy lips. 'You've turned down my proposal but I won't give up. You and I were destined to be together for ever…'

As Sotiris kissed her she breathed a sigh, feeling the sensual arousal deep down inside her spreading to every fibre of her being. How she loved this man! She wasn't going to think about the future. She was going to live for the moment. For tonight, they were simply lovers, desperately in love…and the future could take care of itself…

The sun was shining in through the open window. The heat of it brought Francesca to her senses. It must be later than she'd thought! She would investigate in a moment but meanwhile she didn't want to leave this magic bed. Stretching her legs under the tangled sheet, she wiggled her toes.

Mmm, she felt so alive! Every tiny crevice and section of her skin was still tingling with the wonder of their love-making.

'Come here,' Sotiris reached out with a sensually, languid gesture and drew her back into his arms where she'd lain for most of the night.

'Has last night made any difference to your answer, Francesca?'

Sotiris's husky tone was light but the question was serious. The intense expression in his eyes made it obvious how committed he was to making her change her mind.

'Being with you all through last night was wonderful,' she said slowly, feeling the problems of the real world closing in on her again. 'But I have to be strong and stick to my decision.'

Sotiris gave a deep sigh as he rolled away from her.

Seconds later she heard him in the shower. She was on course again, accepting her inevitable fate…or was she? It was impossible to go back to the way she'd been, but she would try to stick to her resolutions until the end of their affair.

Working in the children's ward later that morning, Francesca was able to put her own problems to the back of her mind. Little Makis smiled happily when she approached his bed.

'Have you heard when am I going to have my transplant, Francesca?'

Francesca smiled as she sat down on the edge of the bed and took hold of Makis's outstretched hand.

'Yes, they phoned from the hospital in Rhodes this morning. It's all fixed for next week. They'd like you and your brother, Niko, to go into hospital tomorrow.'

'Tomorrow, wow! That's great! I'll soon be strong enough to play football with the other children.'

A sad expression suddenly clouded the little boy's face. 'I know you told me you couldn't leave your work here to work at the Rhodes hospital, Francesca, but couldn't you take me over there, make sure the doctors know what they've got to do to Niko and me?'

Francesca squeezed her little patient's hand. 'The doctors at the Rhodes hospital are very clever, Makis, and they've got all the best equipment for looking after you and Niko. That's why you're going to that hospital. Our hospital is small and we wouldn't be able to do the bone-marrow transplant here.'

She hesitated, watching the dull expression in Makis's tired eyes. The last few weeks had been a testing time for him. He'd been thrilled when he'd been told that his twelve-year-old brother was a perfect match for him and that a bone-marrow transplant would go ahead, but he was understandably worried even though he always tried to put on a brave face.

'I'll arrange to come over to the hospital tomorrow with you and Niko, Makis. I won't be able to stay long, but I'll stay long enough to see you and Niko settled in.'

'Oh, thanks, Francesca!' The little boy reached up and kissed her cheek.

Francesca blinked as she tried to remain professional in what was a very touching and poignant moment. She mustn't become too involved with her patient but she couldn't help feeling he was very special to her. How she would feel if this boy was her own child going off for an important operation she simply couldn't imagine!

'Tell me again what's going to happen, Francesca.' Makis fixed his eyes on Francesca's face. 'It's a bit like magic, isn't it, getting rid of my bad bone marrow and putting Niko's good bone marrow there?'

Francesca smiled. 'Yes, you're right, Makis. It is like magic. The doctors on Rhodes will first of all take some blood from Niko. Then a few days later they'll collect some special cells called stem cells from his bone marrow and while they're doing this they'll give him back the blood they took before.'

'Good. I don't want Niko to get sick like me. What bone will they take the stem cells from, Francesca?'

'Most probably from Niko's hip. And then they'll store the cells away until it's time to put them in you.'

'And when they've put the magic cells in me I'll be able to run and jump and—'

'Well, not for a while, Makis.'

She looked up as she heard footsteps coming down

the ward. Sotiris stood quietly at the end of the bed. Makis hadn't noticed he was there.

'Why not?' Makis asked.

Francesca felt unusually nervous with Sotiris listening in. The heightened emotions of their relationship made it difficult to concentrate when he was standing so close to her.

She cleared her throat and gave her little patient her full attention.

'Well, before the doctors can give you Niko's cells, you'll have to spend some time having chemotherapy—that's taking medicine—followed by more time having radiotherapy—that's a kind of X-ray treatment.'

'Why?'

'All this is to get rid of the bad cells in your bone marrow. After that you'll be ready for the doctors to give you Niko's healthy cells.'

'How will they do that?'

'Different doctors have different ideas,' Francesca said carefully. 'They'll probably put them in through a drip like you had soon after you came into hospital here.'

'Oh, good! And then will I be better?'

'The new cells take a few weeks to settle in your bones so the doctors will want you to stay in their hospital until they're happy with the way you're getting better. But as soon as you're strong enough we'll bring you back here and look after you at this hospital.'

Makis smiled. 'Well, that's OK, then. So what time are we going tomorrow, Francesca?'

'In the morning.' Francesca looked up at Sotiris. 'I've promised Makis I'll go over to Rhodes with him and see him and his brother settled in. Can you spare me for half a day?'

Sotiris smiled. 'Are we speaking professionally now, Francesca?'

Francesca could feel a deep blush sweeping over her cheeks. 'Of course.'

'In that case, I'll be happy to rearrange your schedule for tomorrow. But you will hurry back, won't you?'

'I'll do my best.'

'I'll arrange for you to have the helicopter.' Sotiris moved to the head of the bed and sat down beside Makis.

Francesca watched as he spoke quietly to the little boy, reassuring him once more that he was in good hands. Even though Makis didn't know any of the medical staff over on Rhodes, they would soon be good friends just like he and Francesca were.

She could feel a lump rising in her throat. What a wonderful bedside manner Sotiris had with children. What a wonderful father he was with Alex. And what rotten luck that he should have fallen in love with someone who couldn't give him the family life he craved.

She stood up. 'I'll leave you two to get on with your chat. I've got to see some of my other patients.'

Francesca was kept busy throughout the day, treating her small patients. There had been a steady trickle of tourist children throughout the summer brought into the hospital. Most were dealt with in the emergency area but a few had to be admitted. Whenever she was bleeped from the emergency area she left the children's ward and went down there.

This morning she'd been called upon to deal with a near drowning case where a six-year-old who couldn't swim had jumped into the harbour and sunk out of sight for a couple of minutes under a boat. One of the crew from a nearby boat, hearing the screams of horror from the onlookers, had dived in, located the boy, fished him out and managed to revive him.

Francesca had admitted him to the ward. At the end of the afternoon she went back to the little boy's bed to satisfy herself that he was fully recovered.

'You were a lucky boy, Harry,' she said, smiling down at the now perky-looking patient.

Taking hold of his wrist, she checked his pulse. It was absolutely normal now, full, bounding and rhythmical, unlike this morning when it had been difficult to find a pulse. The resilience of youth! She glanced at his charts. Blood pressure and temperature normal.

'You'll be able to leave us tomorrow, Harry.'

The little face creased into a cheeky grin. 'Good. I'm missing my holiday.'

'Just don't go jumping into deep water again.'

'Dad's going to give me swimming lessons. I didn't know the bottom of the sea was so far down. I just wanted to touch it and come up again.'

Francesca ruffled his hair affectionately. 'It was a good thing that sailor had learned how to lifesave. I'll see you tomorrow before you go, Harry.'

'Are you going home now, Francesca?'

'Yes. I'm going to go home and have a nice swim with my two little nieces.'

'How old are they?'

'They're both eight. They're twins, you see.'

'What are their names?'

'Rachel and Samantha.'

Francesca chatted on for a few minutes about where she lived, who she lived with, answering the usual questions that little patients dreamed up when they wanted to apply delaying tactics. It was all part of the healing process, pretending you had all the time in the world when actually you'd had a long day and were dying to go off duty.

A quick goodbye to Makis, more explanations about going to Rhodes tomorrow and she would be away. Just as she escaped out of the building, her mobile phone rang.

'Could you come to my office, Francesca?' Sotiris said. 'I need to explain about the helicopter and when the crew must be back here on the island.'

Somebody else trying delaying tactics! She'd already told Sotiris during the day when they'd been working together in the emergency area how she simply had to spend an evening at home.

'Sotiris, I've already phoned home to say I won't be late. Rachel and Samantha will be down at the water already and—'

'Two minutes, Francesca.'

'Two minutes,' she said, trying to quell the excitement that the sound of his voice always aroused.

The last thing she wanted was to lose her resolution and allow herself to become aroused by being near him.

Sotiris stood up and came round his desk his arms outstretched towards her. For a moment she hesitated before her resolve melted away. The touch of his lips unnerved her resolution further but, reluctantly, she pulled herself away from his arms and began moving back towards the door.

Sotiris watched but didn't try to hold her back. 'I only wanted to see you for a moment. Just to hold you in my arms and kiss you. It's going to be a long night without you.'

She knew exactly how he was feeling. She turned at the door, her hand on the knob.

'I really must go. Manolis will be waiting with the boat down in the harbour. Chloe was off duty today so she spent the day at the house. I arranged to get home as soon as I can to spend the evening with Samantha and Rachel. Chloe is planning to leave them with Mum and me for the night so that she and Demetrius can have a night out by themselves.'

'You didn't tell me anything about this when we were together yesterday evening. When did you arrange all this?'

'Oh, it was a spur-of-the moment thing. I rang home and Chloe said the girls would be thrilled to spend the evening swimming with me and staying the night. Not to mention a romantic evening alone with her husband,' Francesca added quietly.

'That was kind of you, Francesca. I can't help thinking you arranged all this so you wouldn't have to spend another romantic evening with me…'

'Sotiris, you know there's nothing I'd like better than—' She broke off. 'Please, Sotiris, don't make it any harder than it is. Last night was wonderful…too wonderful. We can't go on tearing our hearts out because…'

'OK, I get the message.' He took a step forward, his hand outstretched, thought better of it and remained motionless.

'What was it you wanted to tell me about the helicopter?' Francesca asked.

He gave her a rakish grin. 'Oh, that! I can brief you in the morning. It was only an excuse to get you here. I'd hoped to persuade you out of going home but I can see your mind's made up. You're a very determined woman, Francesca.'

'I've made a promise to my nieces and a promise is a promise. When I really set my mind to something, I try hard to stay on course. It's not always easy.'

A shadow crossed his face. 'I know. Goodbye, Francesca.'

Sotiris sank down into his chair behind the desk as the door closed. It wasn't difficult to recognise the signs. Francesca was trying her hardest to cool off.

But he simply couldn't allow this to happen! Last night as he'd held her in his arms, he'd been sure that she would change her mind. How could anybody kill off a love so precious, the love that the two of them had for each other? It was a unique, precious flower, needing to be nurtured to make it grow, not stamped upon and left to die.

What did it matter that Francesca couldn't have children! Yes, it was sad for both of them. But it wasn't the end of the world. Their love for each other was all that mattered.

Standing up, he paced across the room to the window. Francesca would be getting into the boat soon. He couldn't make out her lovely figure from this angle. She was already swallowed up in the crowds down by the harbour. With a sigh he turned away.

At least he had Alex to return home to. Whatever happened between him and Francesca, he would always have his beloved Alex. But he wanted Francesca as well! He wanted her to be part of their family. He wasn't going to give up easily. Whatever it took, he was going to win her over somehow...

* * *

All the way back across the water, Francesca felt she was being pulled in two different directions. Her heart told her she should be with Sotiris now and for the rest of her life. But her head was telling her she should cool things, somehow find the strength to ease her way out of this wonderful but doomed relationship.

It would be kinder to both of them in the long run if they could end it now. How could they possibly continue at this deep emotional level and then simply break it off and say, enough, that's that, we'll never see each other again?

'You're very quiet this evening, Francesca,' Manolis said, one hand on the wheel as he turned to look at her.

'I'm tired, that's all,' she said quickly, reaching one hand over the side of the boat to trail her hand in the water.

The water was warm even out here at this depth in the bay. The sun had been shining non-stop for weeks and weeks.

'Everything OK at the hospital?'

'Fine.'

She didn't want Manolis to talk to her this evening. Not when her heart was breaking. She leaned back and looked up at the blue sky, now turning red and gold as the sun slipped further down towards the horizon. It was so beautiful, so peaceful out here on the water. She usually enjoyed these journeys to and from home. It was like being in a state of limbo. She could think about how she was going to solve her dilemma but she didn't need to act on anything.

'And Sotiris Papadopoulos, are you still seeing him?'

'Sometimes.'

An understatement, but she couldn't think why Manolis was quizzing her. It was most unusual for him.

'Sotiris is a very good man, Francesca. The Popadopouloses are a good family. Well respected here on Ceres. His father, a wonderful man, much loved on the island, was the mayor for many years and his grandfather before that. I went to the funeral of Constantinos Popadopoulos. Everybody on the island wanted to get into the church. Not a dry eye as the coffin…'

Manolis broke off as his voice choked with emotion.

'Very good people the Popadopoulos family,' he continued, after wiping his eyes with the back of his hand. 'I remember Sotiris when he was a young boy growing up here on Ceres. His big sister, Arwen, only three years older than him, very protective, wouldn't let him out of her sight from the time he was born… What I'm trying to say, Francesca, is that I think you will like him very much.'

'I do like him very much already, but…it's not as simple as that, Manolis.'

Manolis gave a big sigh. 'I understand.'

Francesca was touched by what Manolis had said, but she knew he couldn't possibly understand. Nobody could tell her how to get rid of these unwanted feelings of longing.

CHAPTER EIGHT

COMING home over the bay, Francesca was reminded of that momentous evening three weeks ago when she'd made the effort to begin the cooling-off period between Sotiris and herself. The awful yet necessary strategy seemed to be working but, oh, how heavy her heart felt!

She glanced up at the leaden October sky. It looked a bit like she'd been feeling today as she'd forced herself to stay cheerful with the patients. There wasn't a trace of a sunset this evening. The sky was grey, overcast, the atmosphere still warm but threatening a storm. Autumn weather on Ceres was very unpredictable. One day warm summer weather, the next a sad day like this one which did nothing to raise her spirits.

It was so hard working with Sotiris now at the hospital, watching the pain in his eyes reflect her own, knowing that she mustn't give in. For three weeks he hadn't even asked her out for a friendly drink. Well, an end to their affair was what she'd wanted, wasn't it? She'd been the one who'd insisted they cool off, but it was so hard, so very hard...

'How's it going, Francesca?' Manolis said, his eyes on the sea ahead as he steered towards the shore.

'Fine.'

'That's what you always say.'

She couldn't help smiling. 'That's all you're going to get, Manolis, however hard you fish.'

'I only wanted to tell you that Sotiris came to the

house this afternoon and he was still there when I came over to pick you up.'

So that was where he'd disappeared to after she'd worked with him in the emergency area! One minute he'd been helping her with a suspected cardiac arrest and the next she'd found herself being assisted by Dr Andonis.

Her heart was beating rapidly. Unconsciously, she put a hand to her hair. The wind had ruffled it into a tangled mess. She'd planned to take a shower and wash it back into shape but now....

'Do you think Sotiris will still be there?'

Francesca could feel something akin to panic rising inside her. What did he want? Why had he come to the house?

Manolis pointed across the bay to the car park area in front of the house. 'Sotiris's car is still there. He brought Demetrius with him. The two of them were talking to your father in his study.'

'Curiouser and curiouser,' Francesca muttered under her breath.

Holding the mooring rope, she leapt out onto the jetty and tied up as soon as Manolis pulled the boat near enough.

'Thanks, Manolis.'

She was halfway up the path to the house when she heard Manolis calling, 'Good luck, Francesca!'

She waved a hand, but didn't turn round. Manolis meant well, but every time he started to talk about Sotiris, she could feel a knife twisting inside her. It was like a surgical operation gone wrong. She'd tried to cut a big chunk of her life away and it hadn't worked. She was bleeding inside...

A bit like the operation that had ruined her life.

She increased her pace up the path. Don't think about it now. Just find out what Sotiris wants and try to stay calm. As if she wasn't going through the biggest crisis in her life.

'Francesca!' Her father came out of his study as she reached the top of the stairs. 'We were just talking about you. Come in. I've got Sotiris and Demetrius with me and I was just going to offer them a drink. What would you like, my dear?'

'A glass of water to rehydrate me first, Dad. I'm terribly dry. Then maybe a glass of wine.'

'Go inside.' Her father was holding the study door wide.

She pushed back her tousled hair and forced herself to smile as she went into her father's holy of holies. The smell of the rich leather chairs mingled with the scent of the books that lined the study from floor to ceiling. She was slightly in awe of her father when he was holding court in this room. He seemed to turn back into the eminent surgeon he'd been for so many years.

'Good evening, gentlemen,' she said, with mock formality. 'To what do we owe the pleasure of your company?'

Sotiris and Demetrius were both on their feet, smiling back at her.

Demetrius stepped forward and kissed his sister-in-law on both cheeks. Sotiris remained motionless, his eyes giving nothing away.

Demetrius broke the awkward silence. 'Sotiris is going away to Athens to an important conference next week and he phoned your father to ask his advice about one of the aspects of surgery that will be under discussion.'

'Was my father helpful?'

Francesca sat down in one of the comfy leather armchairs and the two men returned to the upright chairs on either side of her father's desk.

'Professor Metcalfe was most helpful,' Sotiris said evenly. 'He was able to give me a whole new insight into the problem I'll be speaking about in one of my lectures.'

'I'm so glad you found it helpful,' Francesca said politely.

She could feel the dull ache of her longing for Sotiris awakening inside her. He was like a magnet pulling her towards him. His eyes were on her face, dark, enigmatic, but she recognised that beneath his cool, suave exterior he was still smouldering with unexpressed desire as she herself was whenever they were together.

She turned quickly to look at Demetrius. 'Are you going to this conference, Demetrius?'

Demetrius smiled. 'No, I'm going to hold the fort at the hospital. We can't all enjoy the bright lights of Athens. I envy you, Sotiris. The plaka at midnight is fantastic, the food, the wine, the music...magic!'

Francesca could feel the alarm rising inside her. 'And how long will you be away, Sotiris?'

She was trying to take the news calmly but her heart was turning anguished somersaults.

'Oh, only a couple of weeks,' Sotiris said, in a casual tone, deliberately avoiding Francesca's gaze. 'I've appointed Demetrius to be my deputy while I'm away. I've been in touch with Michaelis about this and he insisted that Demetrius was the man for the job of temporary medical director.'

'Did you speak on the phone to Michaelis?'

She was forcing herself to continue as if nothing untoward was happening, but secretly was wondering how she was going to cope. This should have been the answer to her need for a real cooling-off period but it was too harsh to contemplate now that it had been sprung on her so suddenly. Sotiris would be away for two whole weeks. But how would she cope when he went out of her life forever?

Maybe Sotiris wouldn't even return after the conference. Maybe when he got back to the bright lights of Athens he would decide to resume his life at the hospital there. After all, Michaelis was due back on Ceres to resume his post of medical director in November.

She took a deep breath to steady herself. 'How is Michaelis? And Sara?'

'They're fine. Enjoying their work at the hospital in Sydney. They send their love,' Sotiris said.

The door opened. Anthony Metcalfe, smiling benignly, appeared with a tray of drinks. Sotiris sprang to his feet and took the tray from him, setting it down on a table by the window. The older man returned to the chair behind his desk as Sotiris took charge.

'Water for you, Francesca, I believe,' Sotiris said, handing her a large cold glass with ice clinking.

Their fingers touched. It was torture. She looked up into Sotiris's eyes, wishing they were alone together, wishing everyone would go away so that they could make love, here in this room or anywhere so that she could feel his hands caressing her, his body blending with hers...

She put the glass to her lips and drank thirstily. Cold water. A good antidote to rising passion! Almost as good as a cold shower.

Sotiris was opening a bottle of wine, handing out glasses to the others.

'A glass of wine, Francesca?' her father said. 'You've knocked back that water very quickly.'

'Yes, I think I will.'

She took the glass from Sotiris, carefully avoiding all physical contact this time.

'I've got a better idea,' Anthony said with a smile. 'If we've finished our surgical discussion here, let's take our drinks onto the terrace. And then perhaps you gentlemen would like to join us for supper?'

'That's very kind of you, sir,' Sotiris said. 'But I have to get back to my family.'

'Ah, yes, we met your little boy when he came over to play with my granddaughters one day. A lovely child. Remind me of his name.'

'Alex. I shall be leaving him here with my sister when I'm in Athens. Always a terrible wrench for me. I'd like to take him with me but I don't think a four-year-old would be very welcome at the conference.'

Sotiris put his glass down on the table and stood up. Demetrius followed suit, shaking his father-in-law's hand.

'I can't stay either, Anthony. Chloe and the girls have got something planned for this evening.'

'Goodbye,' Sotiris said, moving towards the door. 'Thank you so much for all your help, Professor Metcalfe.'

'You're most welcome. It's good to feel I'm still part of the medical fraternity from time to time.'

Francesca rose to her feet, standing by the door, smiling like a hostess as their guests departed. Her father closed the door and went to sit in an armchair.

'Come and have a chat, Francesca.' He patted the armchair next to him.

She moved across the room and sank back against

the cushions. 'I was going to have a shower, but I'll go in a few minutes. I feel absolutely worn out today. It must be the oppressive weather. I'll feel better when this storm arrives or blows over.'

Her father raised an eyebrow.

'Will you?'

'Will I what?'

'Will you feel better, Francesca? I don't think you'll feel better until you resolve the dilemma of your relationship with Sotiris. What's the problem? You two seemed to be getting on so well, and then suddenly, without any warning, you're home every night, with a face as long as—'

'Dad, it's not as simple as you think.' Francesca swallowed hard. 'You saw the way he spoke so lovingly about his family. Sotiris is a family man. I can't give him children and—'

'But he already has Alex. I think he really loves you. I've watched the way he tried to disguise it this evening but…tell me to stop prying, if you want to, Francesca, but don't you think he's in love with you?'

'He's asked me to marry him.'

She watched the joyful expression flitting across her father's face.

'But I had to say no.'

'Why on earth did you do that?'

'Because I love him too much to see him spoil his own life by being married to a sterile woman.'

'Francesca, no woman is sterile until she has explored every avenue. Surgical techniques are improving all the time. I may be retired but I read a great deal of the current medical literature and I keep myself up to date with what's going on in the surgical world. Sotiris and I were talking just now about advanced improvements in microsurgery and—'

'Dad, I wouldn't want to put Sotiris through the anguish of hoping, only to have his hopes dashed.'

Anthony shook his head. 'You're wrong. I think Sotiris loves you enough to handle hope and disappointment as well as anybody. He's a fine young man, a distinguished surgeon in his own right. How can you deny the pair of you...?'

Francesca stood up before bending down to kiss her father gently on the cheek.

'Thanks, Dad. I'll think about what you said.'

Anthony gave a deep sigh. 'If you want any more advice, I'm always here for you.'

'I've always known that, Dad.' She swallowed hard. 'I remember that day when James Morton said I'd never have children and—'

Anthony pulled himself to his feet and put an arm around his daughter's shoulders.

'Forget what James said when you were sixteen. That's all in the past. You must look to the future.'

Francesca nodded. 'You've given me a lot to think about. I...I'd like to talk to you again about the possibility of surgery, Dad. But, please, not a word to anybody, especially Sotiris. If I did have surgery...and it's a very big if...it would be my own decision. Sotiris mustn't know about it.'

'It would be our secret. I certainly won't say a word. Anyway, Sotiris will be away for a couple of weeks so I'm not likely to see him. But a word of warning, Francesca. A tough, warm-blooded man like Sotiris isn't going to wait around for ever. He'll be looking to the future as well. And having faced one rejection from you...well...'

Anthony spread his hands wide. 'You're not the only woman in the world. He'll be licking his wounds and thinking about starting again soon.'

'Don't Dad, I—'

'There, you see! That scared you, didn't it? You really love that man, don't you? Well, then, you'll have to move fast...'

Francesca was thinking about her father's words as she finished off her ward round at the end of a hot afternoon. Now, at the end of October, the hot weather had returned as a kind of Indian summer and the children's ward, devoid of air-conditioning and open to the garden play area at her request, was too hot today.

Her father's advice still lingered in her mind but it had been impossible to come to a decision. Sotiris was still away at the conference. Another two days before it ended and she didn't know if he would come straight back—or even if he was coming back!

She'd thrown herself into her work with a vengeance, as if to prove to herself that she could go back to her old style of living, just like she'd been before she'd met Sotiris. During the day, absorbed in her work, she'd been OK, but at night... Oh, those long, restless nights, tossing and turning, thinking about Sotiris, wondering what he was doing in Athens, wondering if he'd met someone else, telling herself it didn't matter...

But it did matter! She had to decide soon whether to investigate if surgery would be possible. She might be worrying herself unnecessarily because she could be one of the many cases which were inoperable, but if there was a glimmer of hope, shouldn't she be making plans—?

She went over to Makis's bed. His bone-marrow transplant had been a success so far and she'd gone over to Rhodes the previous week to fly back with him in the air ambulance. But Francesca knew that he would need careful monitoring for some months before they could be sure that the new bone marrow, taken from his brother, wasn't going to react with his own body tissue. He was on carefully controlled anti-rejection medication but Francesca was always on the lookout for signs of graft-versus-host disease, the dreaded complication of bone-marrow transplants.

'How's your tummy feeling, Makis?'

Makis looked up from the book he was reading. He'd been out of bed earlier in the day but had returned for a rest after lunch and stayed there until this evening.

'I've stopped having to run to the toilet, Francesca.'

Francesca smiled. 'Good. I think the extra medicine I gave you has worked, then.'

She certainly hoped so. The diarrhoea that had occurred for a couple of days had worried her. It was one of the symptoms of graft-versus-host disease but there had been no other typical symptoms such as a rash or liver damage. She'd given him a liver-function test and that had been normal.

She put her stethoscope to his chest, listening carefully before running her fingers over his skin. No rash, thank goodness. The diarrhoea had been a false alarm. She could relax again.

Her bleeper went off. She went over to the ward phone. The switchboard told her they had somebody called Arwen on the phone for her. Arwen? Not Sotiris's dreaded sister, surely. Arwen was the last person who would want to contact her. Oh, heavens, had something happened to Sotiris?

'Put her through, please... Hello, yes, this is Dr Francesca.'

'Francesca, I'm sorry to trouble you at the hospital but Sotiris is still away and—'

'Is he all right?'

'Who?'

'Sotiris.'

'Yes, yes, it's Alex I'm worried about. And with Sotiris away I don't know who to turn to. Sotiris is always saying what a good doctor you are and—'

'What's the problem?'

Francesca's relief at knowing that Sotiris was OK was short-lived when she heard that Alex was ill.

'Alex was very restless in the night, then early this morning he said he had a terrible headache. He started being sick. I've kept him in bed all day but he seems to be getting worse. He's very confused and—'

'Could you wrap him up in a blanket and bring him to the hospital, Arwen? Is your husband there to drive you?'

'Yes, Spiros will bring us.'

'I'll be waiting for you in the emergency area.'

'Thank you. Oh, thank you, Francesca.'

Francesca heard the sob as Arwen put the phone down. She had to stay calm. Yes, she was worried about Alex, but she must treat him as any other patient. Stay objective. This mysterious illness could be any number of things. Until she examined Alex she couldn't begin to make a diagnosis.

Arwen hurried straight past reception into the emergency area, quickly followed by Spiros, carrying Alex who was bundled up in a blanket.

'Bring Alex into this cubicle, Spiros,' Francesca said.

The little boy's eyes were shut but as he was lowered onto the examination couch he opened them and stared up at Francesca. He began shaking his head from side to side, moaning softly, gabbling away in a mixture of Greek and English that didn't make sense to anybody. Francesca, in spite of her resolution to stay objective, could feel her alarm rising.

She took Alex's temperature. Dangerously high, although by contrast his pulse was slow. Somewhere at the back of her mind that rang a bell. Her mind was going over other diseases she knew that had this phenomenon.

'You say Alex has been sick, Arwen?'

'Yes, all through the day. And he's had diarrhoea as well.'

As if to prove the point, Alex leaned on his side. Francesca grabbed a vomit bowl and held it under his head just in time. Very little came out, but the poor child retched green, mostly clear fluid in the direction of the bowl.

'I'm going to take Alex along to the children's ward and set up a drip to counteract his dehydration,' Francesca said. 'Arwen, I'm going to be doing lots of tests on Alex to find out exactly what's wrong, so if you and Spiros would like to take a break from looking after him, there's a rest room at the end of the corridor…'

Arwen was blinking back tears. 'Well, Alex doesn't seem to know we're here so it doesn't matter if we leave him.'

'I'll take good care of him.'

'I know you will. That's why I rang you, Francesca. I'm sorry if I...'

Arwen turned away. Spiros put his arm round his wife and led her away.

Francesca was fixing an IV cannula into Alex's wrist. She'd been able to settle him into a side ward away from the rest of the children. With such vaguely disparate symptoms he might be contagious. She couldn't take any chances until she had a firm diagnosis.

Somebody was opening the door. She looked up, ready to turn away anybody who might be unauthorised to be here.

'I'm sorry, but—' She stared. It couldn't be! 'Sotiris? I thought you—'

'Arwen phoned me this morning. Said she was worried. I told her to take Alex to the hospital and contact you. She said she'd see if he improved. Obviously he didn't.'

Francesca turned back to the IV, carefully regulating the flow of glucose and saline solution. Her heart was beating so hard she was sure that Sotiris would hear it.

Sotiris bent over his son and kissed him on the forehead. Alex stirred restlessly but didn't open his eyes. Sotiris swallowed hard. He felt so wretched, so tired, yet in spite of the anguish over his son's condition, still so in love with this impossibly independent woman.

Francesca leaned across the bed and took hold of his hands, looking deep into his eyes. 'It's so hard to be objective when it's your own child, isn't it?'

The touch of her hands made him feel alive again. Oh, how he'd missed her. If only he could take her in his arms...

'I know Alex isn't my child, Sotiris, but I love him as if he were and it's so hard to...'

Sotiris moved swiftly round the bed and without hesitation took her in his arms.

'We both love him,' he whispered as he held her against him. 'He's precious to both of us.' He pulled himself away. 'Now that I'm back, we'll fight this together. Now, let's analyse Alex's symptoms.'

'He's got severe gastroenteritis.'

Sotiris raised an eyebrow. 'We ought to rule out typhoid fever.'

'I've already sent off a sample of Alex's stools for culture at the lab. Alex has a high temperature but a slow pulse. I've sounded his chest and it's a bit wheezy. I've taken a swab of the sputum he coughed up. I've also tested his urine and found traces of albumin.'

Sotiris flinched. 'Albumin? I don't like the sound of that. So what have we got to go on now?'

Francesca took a deep breath. As she tried to stay calm and objective she looked at Sotiris and knew he was feeling exactly the same. It was almost as if this was their child who was dangerously ill.

'We've got symptoms of enteritis that might be typhoid fever,' she began in a quiet voice. 'Except the onset was very sudden. High temperature, slow pulse, restlessness bordering on delirium at times, albuminuria...'

The door was opening again. Francesca moved towards it. 'I'm sorry but—Oh, Arwen it's you.'

'Sotiris!' Arwen embraced her brother. 'I'm so glad you're here. Spiros thinks we should go home to the children. Mother came round to look after them but she just phoned to say she'll have to go home. Joey the parrot is playing up again, keeping everybody on the street awake with its dreadful croaky shrieking. It's been like this for a few days and—'

'That's it!' Francesca clasped her hands together. 'Arwen, has the parrot always had a croaky voice?'

'Well, not until recently. I think it must be getting old or something. I've told Mother she ought to get rid of it. She's always having to clear up its dreadful mess when she lets it fly around the house and—'

'Psittacosis!' Francesca said. 'The parrot has psittacosis, which can be passed on to human beings. Has Alex been round to see your mother recently, Arwen?'

She looked bewildered. 'Well, of course he has. He practically lives there when—Oh, dear. It's serious, isn't it?'

'Yes, it's serious, but now we've got a diagnosis it's treatable,' Sotiris said.

'I'm sure I'm right,' Francesca said, mentally reviewing the symptoms. 'I had a case like this in London quite recently. Tetracyline, that's the antibiotic that cured my little patient.'

'I'll get some,' Sotiris said.

'My other patient responded very quickly to tetracycline,' Francesca told Arwen. 'If I've got the right diagnosis, by this time tomorrow we should see a definite improvement.'

Alex was sitting up in bed propped against pillows when Francesca got back to his side ward from her other duties in the hospital. It had been a long day and, having had very little sleep as she'd kept watch in a chair near Alex's bed the night before, she was feeling unusually tired. Alex's little face creased into a grin when he saw her.

'Dad said I gave you all a scare yesterday.'

Francesca sank down onto the side of his bed. 'Yes, you certainly did. How are you feeling now, Alex?'

'I'm not sure. My legs were a bit wobbly when I went to the toilet and my head's a bit fuzzy but everything else is OK. Can I go home?'

Sotiris, coming in, answered for her. 'In a few days, Alex. We need to keep you here till we're absolutely sure you're better. Anyway, Francesca and I will be coming in to see you a lot. Last night I was in that chair over there and Francesca was in this chair here, but we're not going to do that tonight. Arwen said she'd like to stay with you tonight.'

As if on cue, Arwen poked her head around the door. 'I've brought that book we were reading together, Alex.'

'Great! Can you start at the place where the green dragon...?'

Arwen winked at her brother. 'Sotiris, you may go off duty now, and that's an order.'

'Always bossing me around, my big sister,' Alex said, as he dropped a kiss on his sister's head. 'Goodnight, Alex.'

'Oh, goodnight, Dad, goodnight, Francesca. Arwen, you know the bit I mean. There's fire coming out of the dragon's nose and...'

In the corridor, Sotiris put his arm round Francesca's shoulders. All the previous night he'd been longing to say something to her, to find out if she'd changed her mind, but as they'd slumbered in Alex's room, in chairs on opposite sides of the bed, their only concern had been for Alex. Now he wanted to clear the air. He felt as if he'd left under a cloud.

'We need to talk, Francesca,' Sotiris said. 'Come home with me and I'll cook supper.'

'Home? Is it OK for me to be seen there with you?' she joked. 'You've never asked me home before.'

Sotiris gave her a wry smile. 'Arwen would have scratched your eyes out but it seems you two are great friends now.'

'It's amazing how a crisis can draw people together.'

'Yes.' Sotiris took his arm from Francesca's shoulder as they began to walk side by side along the corridor.

He wasn't sure how she was feeling about him at all or if anything had changed while he'd been away.

'When I got back last night and saw you with my son, Francesca, I just…' His voice choked. He'd been going to say how much he loved her but this wasn't the place. Later, at home, when they were truly alone.

Francesca put down her coffee-cup and faced Sotiris across the supper table.

'That was a delicious omelette, Sotiris.'

'I'm glad you enjoyed it.'

How formal this all was. He didn't know how he was going to thaw out the atmosphere. Since bringing Francesca back home, she'd seemed so withdrawn, so unapproachable. There was something on her mind and it wasn't what he'd hoped for. Somebody had once told him that the English had a saying about absence making the heart grow fonder. That didn't seem to be happening—yet.

There was still time. He reached for the bottle of wine to top up Francesca's glass but saw that she hadn't even touched the first glass.

'Francesca, there's something I want to say. While

I was away from you, I had time to think...about us. And when I got back, when I saw you with Alex, so right for him as a mother, so perfect as a wife for me...well, what will it take for me to convince you that I don't care about not having more babies? All I want is you, Francesca. I love you. I've never loved like this before and I can't go on unless you reconsider my proposal.'

He gazed at her with imploring eyes that tore at her heartstrings.

She swallowed hard, leaning back in her chair, looking up at the high ceiling, the typical Greek moussandra, the cottage atmosphere, the warm, cosy ambience that surrounded her whenever she was with Sotiris. She could live here with him if only she could rid herself of the idea that it wouldn't be enough for Sotiris. Sooner or later he might decide he wanted more than she could give.

'Sotiris, I've had time to think this through while you've been away and I've come to a decision. It's all or nothing with me. I can't give you second best and so—No, hear me out—'

She put up her hand as if to shield herself from his questions so that she could crystallise her own thoughts. It was only since he'd returned early yesterday evening that her course of action had become clear.

'I've been discussing the problem of my sterility with my father. He's convinced me that I should go ahead and find out if my Fallopian tubes could be unblocked. He has a friend, Paul Collins, a former student of his, now an eminent consultant gynacologist who specialises in microsurgery. Paul has his own nursing home in—'

'In London,' Sotiris interrupted quietly. 'I know. I've

actually been there to see some of the work Paul is doing. He's extremely well respected in his field. But when are you planning to go to London?'

She drew in her breath. 'At the beginning of November. I checked with Michaelis on the phone a couple of days ago to see if I could leave Ceres hospital. My contract ends in November. Michaelis said if it was OK with you, he was agreeable.'

'It's really not necessary to go through all this for me, Francesca. I couldn't possibly love you any more than I do. Please, marry me, and then later if you feel the need to have this operation then—'

'As I said, it's all or nothing with me,' she repeated slowly, her eyes lingering over his much-loved face. 'If Paul Collins can't effect a cure for my childlessness, I'll simply stay on in London and resume my hospital work there. It was very fulfilling before…before… Oh, Sotiris, I'm so scared to build up my hopes, only to have them dashed. That's what I've always been afraid of. That's why I've never even considered the possibility that…'

Sotiris's arms were round her. He was kissing her face, her hair, her neck, while his soothing hands were caressing her, trying to calm her fears, telling her everything would be all right. All they needed was each other. It didn't matter what the outcome was…

She was dimly aware that Sotiris was carrying her up the stairs, laying her down on a soft, feather mattress, stroking her hair, murmuring soothing words to her. And all the while she was clinging to him, not wanting him ever to leave her again…

Francesca stirred in Sotiris's arms. She could hear a cock crowing over on the hillside beyond the house.

Sotiris's bedroom was bigger than she remembered last night. Cretonne curtains, bookshelves, large oak furniture lovingly polished by one of his sisters, she suspected, or his mother. Sotiris had his own large extended family. She shouldn't feel bad about not being able to give him more children.

But she would feel bad. She would never forgive herself. That was why, having made the decision, she must go through with her plan. No woman was sterile until she'd explored every avenue, her father had said.

'Come back to bed,' Sotiris said sleepily as she put her feet to the floor.

He reached out for her but she was too quick for him. Her body was tingling with the memories of last night—the caresses, the feeling that she was floating in outer space, that only the two of them existed in their own idyllic paradise. But this was where it must end until she could be sure that she could create the whole dream for the two of them.

'I want to go into hospital to see my patients, check that they're all going to be OK. Then I'm going to home to make some phone calls, book myself on a flight for the first of November if possible...'

'You're really going through with it, aren't you, Francesca?'

'Yes, my mind's made up. And, Sotiris, if the operation isn't successful and I stay on in London, remember it's because I loved you too much and I want you to be happy for the rest of your life...without me...'

'Don't say that. I love you.' Sotiris sprang out of bed and took her in his arms. For a moment she allowed herself the joy of leaning against him, savouring the feel of his lips on hers, before she pulled away.

'Come on, I'll drive you into hospital,' Sotiris said in a resigned tone.

CHAPTER NINE

'THERE you are, Francesca, as good as new.' The bright-eyed nursing sister stood back to admire her handiwork before asking, 'Would you like a cup of tea now?'

Francesca smiled. 'Yes, please.' She glanced at the clock. 'Four o'clock on the dot, Ellen. I can tell I'm back in England.'

Ellen smiled. 'You didn't feel a thing when I took the stitches out, did you?'

'It was completely painless. Just like my operation last week.'

'Oh these new microsurgery techniques are amazing. Especially when Paul is in charge. Why, I remember only a few years ago when...'

She broke off, smiling as a tall, fair-haired man entered Francesca's private room. 'Talk of the devil. I was just telling Francesca about how microsurgery has improved since I first started nursing. Cup of tea, Paul?'

'Yes, please, Ellen. I need something to warm me up. It's freezing cold and raining out there. I've just driven through the heavy traffic in central London. November has got to be the worst month of the year. Now, how's my patient? You were careful not to spoil that tiny scar I made, weren't you, Ellen? I expect Francesca will be sunning herself on a Greek beach in her bikini again soon.'

'Lucky girl,' Ellen said, closing the door behind her.

'Well, I'm not sure I'll be going back straight away,' Francesca said carefully. 'It's going to depend on—'

She broke off. Someone was tapping on the door. Paul stood up to open it but Ellen coming along the corridor outside, had beaten him to it.

'A visitor for you, Francesca,' she announced, placing a cup of tea on her bedside table before turning to look at the tall, dark, handsome visitor. 'Would you like a cup, sir?'

Sotiris shook his head. 'No, thanks, Sister.'

'Well, you can just sit here and chat, then.' The helpful sister drew up another chair.

Sotiris sat down, his eyes on Francesca. 'I know you asked me not to come, but I simply had to know how you are. I was hoping for a phone call, or perhaps to be allowed to put my own phone calls through to your room. But I was told that you didn't want to speak to anybody, so...'

'I feel OK, Sotiris. I don't know how successful the operation has been and until I know...well...' She broke off.

Sotiris knew exactly what she meant. The stubborn woman hadn't changed! He turned to look at Paul.

'I'm Sotiris Popadopoulos. We met at a surgical conference here in London some time ago.'

Paul smiled. 'Yes, I remember you very well now. I enjoyed your talk—most enlightening.' He hesitated. 'Forgive me, but where do you fit into Francesca's life. Are you...?'

'Sotiris is a colleague at Ceres hospital and a very good friend,' Francesca said.

Paul cleared his throat. 'I just wondered if Sotiris might be the man who persuaded you to have the operation. There's usually a reason why my patients with extensive abdominal scarring decide to have their tubes unblocked after accepting sterility for a few years.'

Sotiris leaned forward, his eyes keen. 'So you think you've successfully unblocked Francesca's Fallopian tubes, do you, Paul?'

The surgeon glanced at Francesca. 'Do you mind if I discuss your case with Sotiris?'

'No, I'm happy for Sotiris to know what's happened. But, please, don't raise his hopes too much because…'

Paul was smiling. 'Ah, so I was right about Sotiris being an important man in your life, Francesca.'

She blushed but couldn't think of anything to say in reply as she waited for Paul to elaborate on the intricacies of her operation.

'I performed a cornual anastomosis using microsurgery,' Paul said.

Sotiris nodded. 'So you removed the blocked part of the tubes and stitched the remainder back onto the original openings. Not really my field, but I've read about it. Isn't it difficult technically and fairly time-consuming?'

'Exactly! But the surgical effort is worth it, particularly as the success rate in terms of live births afterwards is very high. All my patients are different. Some want to have sexual intercourse immediately after they've had their stitches out—and there's absolutely no reason why they shouldn't. You can't do any damage to the tubes now. Other patients—'

'Excuse me,' Francesca said, putting her teacup down on the bedside table. 'Do you think you might include me in this conversation? I know I'm only the patient, but nobody's asked me how I feel about babies. I might want to carry on with my career, childless and unburdened with domestic life or…'

She watched the slow smiles spreading across the faces of the two surgeons.

'Unlikely!' Paul said.

'And it would be very ungrateful of you, considering the time that Paul has invested in unblocking your tubes,' Sotiris said.

Francesca couldn't stop herself from smiling now. 'OK, I give in. Yes, I do want a baby. Of course I want a baby! So, tell me, Paul, how soon will I know if I'm fertile or not? What kind of tests would—?'

'The best test would be to make love frequently and then report back to me for a pregnancy test if you miss a period. I remember one patient who came for a pregnancy test just six weeks after I'd operated on her to unblock her tubes.'

Sotiris leaned forward. 'And?'

Paul smiled. 'Oh, the test was positive. Mother and baby are doing fine. They often call in to see me. She's expecting her second baby.'

The surgeon stood up, still smiling. 'I'm going to keep you here for another day, Francesca. But there's no reason why Sotiris can't stay as well...'

The implication hung in the air as Paul closed the door firmly behind him.

Sotiris turned to Francesca. 'Are you really feeling OK?'

'Never better.'

Sotiris gave her a rakish grin. 'In the interests of science, don't you think we ought to start your post-operative tests?'

Francesca held out her arms towards him. 'I've got a very scientific feeling deep down inside me. I could try to stifle it but...'

Sotiris was holding her firmly against him, his lips

hovering close to hers. He breathed a deep sigh. 'I've missed you so much, Francesca. Don't ever leave me again will you?'

'We'd better check on whether—'

Sotiris caressed her lovingly. 'I told you, I don't care, but let's make love anyway. I've been too long without you.'

Outside in the corridor, Paul intercepted his industrious sister as she approached Francesca's door, intent on clearing the teacups.

'Where did we put that "Do Not Disturb" sign, Sister?' he was asking.

Ellen smiled conspiratorially. 'Hoping to improve your surgical success rate, Paul?'

'I'm hoping this couple might give me a world record,' he said amiably, as he fixed the sign on their door. 'From the positive vibes I detected between the two of them, I should say we're in with a chance.'

It was strange, waking up with Sotiris lying beside her. Francesca switched on the bedside light. Outside the double-glazed windows she could see and hear the rain pelting down from the dark night sky. She looked around at the white walls, the clean, aseptic, functional furniture, the pastel blue curtains tied back against the sides of the two windows that overlooked the nursing-home garden.

As she looked lovingly down at Sotiris, she listened for a moment to his gentle breathing. There was a smile on his face as if he was dreaming. Maybe he was reliving the past few hours they'd spent in each other's arms. She felt a tingling, tantalising sensation running through her.

Sotiris opened his eyes and reached out towards her.

She moved into the circle of his arms, resting her head on his shoulder.

'What a perfect way to make a baby,' he whispered, his voice still husky with passion.

'Mmm... Before the operation I thought I mightn't be interested in making love for ages but...'

'But you were wrong, weren't you?'

She felt his arms tightening around her. 'How are you feeling now? Do you think we should make sure?'

'I think I ought to find out what's happening here at the nursing home. I can't think why we've been left alone so long.'

Sotiris smiled. 'I can! He's a very wise surgeon, Mr Paul Collins. He doesn't want to spend hours giving you back your fertility if it's just going to go to waste.'

'Let me check what's happening.' She picked up the bedside phone.

Sotiris leaned across. 'Tell Sister we tried our best to—'

'Shh! Hello, Ellen. I was just wondering...'

'Ah, you're awake, Francesca. How are you feeling?'

'Wonderful! Never better.'

'Good. Well, you'll be wanting some supper now, I expect.' Ellen reeled off the possibilities on the menu.

'Something light, I think. The cold chicken salad sounds lovely.'

'And will Mr Popadopoulos be staying for supper?'

Sotiris was nodding his head as he climbed out of bed and made for the shower room.

'Yes, supper for two, please.'

'Your parents phoned, Francesca,' Ellen continued. 'I told them I couldn't put any phone calls through as you were asleep, so they're going to phone tomorrow.'

'Thank you.'

Francesca lay back against her pillows, listening to the sound of the shower cascading over Sotiris's virile body. What a man! And, oh, how happy she felt to be with him again. There was only one tiny doubt in her mind.

Supposing that she was still unable to have a baby. Nothing would have changed then, would it? Her love would still be strong, but she must make it clear to Sotiris that she wouldn't hold him against his will.

As they ate their supper, sitting at the small table by the window, Sotiris fully dressed again, Francesca in a white towelling robe, the unanswered question continued to trouble her. As soon as the maid had been in to clear away their trays and leave them with their coffee, Francesca broached the subject.

'Sotiris, I'm hoping that I'm able to have children but if the worst comes to the worst...'

'I know what you want to tell me but, please, don't.'

Sotiris got up, coming round the back of her chair to help her to her feet. She remained quiet until he'd escorted her gently to one of the armchairs. Sitting close beside her in another chair, he took hold of her hands.

'You are the most precious person in the world to me,' he said, his voice full of emotion. 'Alex is precious, too, but Alex will grow up and leave me, whereas you and I could be together for the rest of our lives. I want you to be my wife, Francesca. I don't care if we have other babies or not...truly, babies are not as important as you are to me. Please, Francesca...'

He was on his knees now, both hands pressed together as if he was praying.

'Please, Francesca, will you marry me?'

She looked at the love of her life, his thick dark hair, his expressive handsome face, his gorgeous body, and finally she was convinced that he meant what he'd said. He was an honest man through and through and she had to believe that he would be faithful to her even if she was still unable to give him the family he wanted.

'Yes, I'll marry you, Sotiris,' she said quietly.

She would never forget this moment in her life. The look of shock on Sotiris's face was something that would always stay with her. First there was the expression of shock, followed immediately by radiant happiness.

He drew her towards him, his kiss infinitely tender. 'I love you, Francesca,' he whispered.

'And I love you, Sotiris.'

There were tears threatening to spill out of her eyes. Why did people always have this urge to cry when there was a wedding in the offing? A wedding... The enormity of what she'd taken on hit her. Weddings, family, guests...

'Sotiris, we needn't rush into a wedding, need we? I mean, it's the middle of winter and—'

'It's not the middle of winter in Ceres. It's not even the middle of November.'

Sotiris was back in his chair now, leaning back against the cushions, his hand stretched across to cling to Francesca's as if he intended never to release her.

'When I left Ceres this morning, the sun was shining on the hills. Yesterday, Alex and I were swimming down at the beach house and the sea was still warm. The sun has been shining all through the summer and the water retains its heat until Christmas.'

'Oh, Sotiris, I'm so looking forward to going home to Ceres. When you were talking about it just now, I was remembering the scent of the herbs on the hill above the beach house, the lemon trees, the wild flowers…'

'We'll go back in a couple of days. I'll arrange everything—flights, wedding plans, rings…'

'Sotiris. I'd love to go back soon, but couldn't the wedding plans wait until the spring?'

Sotiris smiled. 'No. As you say in England, I've got to make an honest woman of you. And the sooner the better.'

Francesca laughed. 'That's hopelessly outdated.'

'I know. That was only my excuse to make you agree with me. The thing is, if we were to marry in, say, a couple of weeks…'

'A couple of weeks!'

'We could have all your family at the wedding. Michaelis and Sara have come back from Australia. But they intend to return in three weeks' time when they've sorted things out on Ceres.'

'They're going to return to Australia? But what about—?'

'Michaelis and Sara have decided to spend two years working in Australia. They enjoyed their temporary work at the hospital in Sydney and they've both been offered permanent posts on the medical staff. So they came home a couple of days ago and started sorting out their affairs. Michaelis has taken over from me at the hospital while I'm away. That's why if I could organise a wedding in the Popadopoulos family church…'

'Tell me about this church,' Francesca said, a trifle nervously.

'It's the small chapel on the island, up on the hill

behind the beach house. I took you there one day, remember?'

'Yes, I remember now. Up there on the hillside. Why do you call it the family church?'

'It's a long story. Many years ago there were several families living on the island. Sponge fishing was the main source of income. Little by little as it grew less profitable the people drifted away. When my father bought the ruined house by the shore that he turned into our beach house, he also restored the old church. Since then the Popadopoulos family have made sure that the chapel hasn't fallen into disrepair.

'As a family we arrange the upkeep of the church. It's rarely used now. Mostly for family weddings and so on. But for many years our family has maintained it, arranged for it to be regularly cleaned, for the candlesticks to be polished, the stained-glass windows kept in good order and so on My sisters arrange the cleaning now, so I don't know exactly how they manage it.'

'I remember thinking it was so wonderful to find such a beautiful chapel with fresh flowers and... Oh, but Sotiris, how would we get the wedding guests there?'

'Francesca, let me worry about the logistics of the day. All you've got to do is agree to the idea that we will marry in about two weeks' time.'

Francesca smiled. The excitement of what was going to happen soon had finally got through to her.

'If this was going to happen in England, there would be panic stations in the Metcalfe family. Everybody would be worrying about taxis, guests lists, caterers, the weather...but if I put myself into Ceres mode I'll be able to take a more relaxed view.'

'Was that a yes?'

Francesca gave a sigh of pure happiness. 'It certainly was.'

'Great!'

As Sotiris jumped to his feet, Francesca thought how much he resembled his son when he was excited about something. She could see the facial expressions Sotiris would have had when he was a boy. How wonderful it would be to create another child with this man!

Unconsciously she placed her hands over her abdomen. Was there anything happening there at the moment?

'You're looking very solemn all of a sudden, darling.' Sotiris leaned over her. 'Are you feeling OK?'

'I'm fine!' She smiled. 'Never better.'

'You must go back to bed now. Doctor's orders.' He grinned. 'Not what you think. I have to go back to the hotel. I need to make phone calls, do some paperwork, set the wheels in motion for the wedding. But now I want you to sleep. You must take all the rest you can so that you'll look radiant on our wedding day.'

'There's just one thing that's been worrying me, Sotiris.'

Sotiris froze. Surely after all they'd been through together, Francesca couldn't change her mind now...or could she?

'Yes?' he enquired.

'Whatever happened to the parrot?'

'The parrot?' Sotiris felt nothing but relief. 'I thought you were going to find another obstacle to the plans. Joey was taken to the vet. The vet put him in isolation while he was being treated for his psittacosis—mainly diarrhoea and a sore, croaky throat—and Joey's now free from the disease.'

'So is he back with your mother again?'

Sotiris shook his head. 'Oh no. My mother didn't want him back. Not if he was going to have a bad effect on her grandchildren. Fortunately none of her other grandchildren had spent as much time with the parrot as Alex had so we haven't had any more scares in the family. The vet found a good home for Joey when he'd recovered so everybody's happy again.'

Francesca smiled. 'I like a happy ending. Just one more thing, Sotiris, before you go…'

'Yes?'

'How's Makis? Is he still on the children's ward?'

'I discharged our little patient last week. The bone-marrow transplant has been a definite success and he's fighting fit. No complications at all. He'll be coming back to outpatients for check-ups, of course, so we shan't lose touch with him.'

'Another success story.'

'And now, Francesca, will you let me help you back to bed and will you promise to stop thinking and go to sleep?'

He tucked her up as if she was a child, leaning over to kiss her very gently before tiptoeing out of the door.

'Sleep well, my darling. Pleasant dreams.'

Francesca lay back against the pillows after Sotiris had gone. She was luxuriating in her happiness. Her head was spinning with wedding plans but Sotiris had advised her to rest and that was what she was going to do—for tonight.

Tomorrow, when her mother heard there was to be another wedding in the family…well, that was when the fun would start!

CHAPTER TEN

FRANCESCA looked out across the sea that was reflecting the deep blue of the sky. Not a cloud was in sight on this, her special day, her wedding day. She lay back against the side of the wooden seat. Her mother had advised her to stay in the cabin so that she wouldn't spoil her dress, but Francesca wasn't about to miss a moment of this lovely day. Two weeks of England in November had made her appreciate all the more how lucky she was to live on an island like Ceres.

'You're sure you're not too cold out here, Francesca?'

Francesca smiled at Chloe. 'I'm as warm as toast. It's taken me two weeks to thaw out since I came back from England but I'm well and truly warmed through now.'

'Your dress looks lovely, shining in the sun,' Sara said, coming out of the cabin. 'I was a bit worried this morning when I saw Maria ironing all that lace but she's obviously done it before.'

'She ironed both our dresses for our double wedding in August, Sara, remember?'

Sara smiled. 'It seems a lifetime ago. So much has happened since then.'

'You can say that again!' Francesca said. 'When I came out here to your wedding in August I was so unhappy, so... Honestly, I can't believe I'm the same person now.'

'Neither can we,' Sara said, sitting down beside her sister.

Chloe joined her on the other side. Both sisters unconsciously smoothed out the folds of Francesca's dress.

'You're not getting marks on your dress, are you, Francesca?' Pam came out of the cabin, gazing fondly at all three of her beautiful daughters. 'My, what a lovely sight. I must have a picture of this.'

'I've got my little camera at the bottom of my bag somewhere. Ah, here it is. You know, I've already written up a description of your dresses for your aunt Mary in America who can't make it because of her arthritis. I've described Francesca's in detail, the lace tiers over the full, floor-length silk skirt, the sweetheart neckline that looks so lovely with my mother's silver necklace round the throat...

'Keep still, girls! OK, you can relax now. And I've said that Sara and Chloe in cream satin, floor-length, fitted skirts and bodices with masses of covered buttons to do up... I think I'll need another picture to show off the dresses... You won't forget to put the flower headdresses on when we get there, will you?'

As their mother focussed her camera on them, all three of them prepared for the required pose.

'Smile!' Pam called brightly, gaily, just as she had done throughout the years since they were small toddlers. 'Another one for the new album...or rather albums. They're filling up rapidly. It's a good thing I haven't any more daughters.'

'It'll be the granddaughters' weddings before you know where you are, Mum,' Chloe said. 'Talking of which, are they OK?'

'Manolis is teaching them how to steer the boat,'

Pam said. 'Now, let me have another picture in case those don't come out properly...'

Several more pictures were taken before Pam retired back to the cabin.

'That dressmaker on the other side of the island made a wonderful dress for you,' Chloe said admiringly. 'She was brilliant to do it in such a short time. Not to mention our matron-of-honour creations.'

'I think her daughters helped this time,' Francesca said, putting her hand on the nipped-in waist. 'That feels a bit tight here but I'll breathe in.'

Sara smiled. 'Maybe you're putting on weight.'

'Not yet, surely!' Francesca grinned. 'I mean...'

'Well, that's a pregnant pause if ever there was one,' Chloe said before they all burst out laughing.

'I'm living in hope,' Francesca said. 'Give me time. It's less than a month since my operation but it's not for want of trying.'

'Sara, tell us about your honeymoon travels,' Chloe said, thinking it was time to change the delicate subject.

'Oh, it was magic! Singapore, Thailand, Hong Kong, so many exotic places. But Australia was amazing. The variety of different areas. You'd need a lifetime to see that country properly. That's one reason we're going back. We're going to continue working in this super hospital in Sydney and in our holiday times we'll hire a camper van and travel around.'

'Sounds wonderful!' Francesca said.

'It is. I'm glad that Sotiris has agreed to stay on at the hospital as medical director to replace Michaelis permanently.'

Francesca smiled. 'It's all working out beautifully. Sotiris has resigned from his position in Athens but he's agreed to go back occasionally for consultations. We both know that Alex adores living here on Ceres.'

'Especially now that he's going to have you and Sotiris with him all the time,' Sara said. 'Does Alex mind leaving Arwen?'

'The transition has been easy. He'll live with us in Sotiris's house...'

'Your house,' Chloe corrected, with a smile.

'Our house, but he'll be part of the larger extended family that live on Constantinos Street. There's a wonderful warm family atmosphere up there.'

'Don't you think you might feel swamped by so many of Sotiris's family?' Sara asked cautiously.

Francesca shook her head. 'No, I get on well with all of them...now,' she added with a wry grin. 'Arwen was a bit difficult when I first started seeing Sotiris but we've been the greatest of friends ever since she brought Alex into hospital with psittacosis.'

'Is Alex completely over that now?' Chloe asked.

'He's extremely fit. We have a great time together. I enjoyed my first week back from England when I lived in Sotiris's house—our house. Sotiris wanted me to be sure I would be happy there, surrounded by so many of his family.'

Francesca smiled as she remembered how loving and supportive Sotiris had been in that first week out of hospital, plunged as she had been into the bosom of his family.

'Sotiris said if I found his family too overwhelming he would be happy to buy a house somewhere else on the island. But I knew it was better for Alex to stay near the family he'd grown up with. It was strange, moving back home to Nimborio for this last week, but

I'd promised to be there to give Mum a hand before the wedding.'

An aeroplane was climbing steeply up into the sky from Rhodes airport just across the water. The white contrail contrasted beautifully with the blue of the sky.

'Doesn't that look like a bridal train to you?' Francesca asked her sisters.

They both smiled. 'Only if bridal trains are on your mind,' Sara said. 'I'll give you a hand, fixing it to the back of your belt, when we're ashore.'

'And I'll make sure Rachel and Samantha hold your train up off the ground and don't step on it,' Chloe said.

'Thanks. Now, where was I? Oh, yes, last week with Mum. In the event, there wasn't much to do, apart from contacting some of our relatives and friends about the wedding and have fittings for my dress. So Mum and I had a nice cosy week together. Dad had to go over to Rhodes for a couple of days to give a lecture to some medical students. Sotiris insisted on making all the arrangements for the church, the reception at the beach house and so on.'

'And Sotiris's mother? Does she approve of his choice of bride?' Chloe asked.

'Oh, she's adorable. Such a wicked sense of humour.'

'I'm glad you're so happy,' Sara said. 'Will you be too busy to keep going down to check on our house like you have been doing while we were away?'

'Of course we'll keep an eye on the place.'

'Thanks, and, please, if you ever need to get away from the in-laws, regard it as your second home, won't you?'

Francesca laughed. 'I'm afraid we already have been

doing just that. It was a very valuable hide-away when you were away, Sara.'

'Good! Hey, it looks like we're almost there,' Sara said. 'Just look at the boats behind us. It's like the Armada. I can't count how many there are. They're all waiting for the bride's boat to tie up first, but it looks as if the bridegroom's party have settled into the harbour already.'

'Oh, look at the balloons on the jetty!' Francesca said.

'And the streamers on the hillside!' Rachel cried as she came out of the cabin, closely followed by Samantha.

'Don't the twins look lovely in pink?' Francesca said.

'Come here, girls,' Chloe called. 'I need to fix your head dresses.'

'Sara, will you fix mine?' Francesca asked, suddenly feeling as if butterflies were flapping around in her tummy. 'My fingers are all thumbs.'

'Come in the cabin. There's a mirror there.'

Francesca looked at the face in the mirror as Sara fixed the final pin into her long blonde hair. The antique headdress worn by Sotiris's grandmother on her wedding day was more like a tiara. Someone had lovingly polished the silver so that it shone and the small diamonds set in the headband sparkled in the warm sunlight.

She swallowed the lump in her throat. The boat had gone quiet. Everyone was already on shore except herself and her younger sister, Sara.

'Did you feel like this on your wedding day, sis?' she asked in a small voice.

'Like what?' Sara asked gently.

'Oh, so happy...but, oh, so scared...'

Sara reached for Francesca's hand, clasping it firmly.

'Do you know, that's the first time I've ever known you to admit to being scared, Francesca? You've always been there for me when I needed you, my big sister. Nothing was ever too difficult for you... Yes, I did feel scared, but as soon as I saw Michaelis I was fine. Come on, Sotiris will be waiting for you and then you'll forget all about your nerves...'

Sotiris was waiting at the top of the hill on the wide path leading to the chapel and it was just like Sara had told her it would be. Her nerves vanished as she saw him walking towards her.

They'd departed from the usual Ceres island tradition of having the bride and groom coming to meet each other in a procession from their own respective houses. Sotiris had jokingly pointed out a couple of days ago that this would have proved totally impracticable unless they agreed to meet somewhere out at sea. And there was a danger their boats might collide in the swell of the waves!

Francesca had agreed that she would go along with whatever Sotiris decided and he'd come up with the idea that he and some close family members would arrive on the island first, go up the path towards the church and then return to meet the bridal party when they saw Francesca walking up the path.

Sotiris saw her first, but it was Alex who broke away and came dashing down the path with outstretched arms.

'Francesca! You look like a princess. Are you really a princess?'

'Only for today, Alex.'

She bent down and joined in the affectionate hug and the sloppy kiss on the cheek that removed the remains of the make-up that hadn't already dissolved away in the spray from the sea. At that moment she felt as if she could never be happier in her life.

But she was wrong! Because the tall, dark, handsome, intensely desirable bridegroom who was now taking her in his arms, disregarding all onlookers and completely oblivious to tradition, was transporting her somewhere up onto cloud nine.

She opened her eyes as Sotiris's sensual kiss lightened.

'I'm getting married to the most beautiful woman in the world today,' he whispered.

She smiled up into his tender eyes. 'That's a coincidence. Because I'm getting married to the most wonderful—'

'Daddy, Francesca, come on! Let's go and get married.'

They both laughed as Alex tugged at the coat tails of Sotiris's dark suit with one hand and Francesca's precariously attached train with the other.

Francesca reached down and took hold of Alex's hand. 'Come on, Alex. Can you show me the way to the wedding?'

'It's up there Francesca. Can you see that white chapel? There's an enormous man inside called a priest. He's got a big beard, and he's very old, with a deep voice like this...'

Alex tried to make a noise that sounded more like a dragon to the twins holding onto Francesca's train. They dissolved into fits of laughter and had to be replaced for a few seconds by Chloe who stepped into the breach and secured the bridal train firmly in place under Francesca's belt.

Francesca, one hand held by Sotiris and one by Alex, walked into the small chapel. The smell of the incense, the cool interior, the icons and statues looking down at her, the priest and his assistant waiting to start the ceremony... She didn't feel nervous. She felt excited. This was the happiest day of her life and she would most probably bore her grandchildren rigid with tales of how...

If she ever had any children, that was... No, she mustn't think about that. Nothing was going to spoil her big day. She had everything in the world she could possibly wish for...except...

Sotiris stooped down to speak to Alex. 'Alex, would you like to go and sit with Arwen now?'

Alex smiled an angelic smile as he clung on tightly to Francesca's hand. 'I'd rather stay with Francesca, Dad. I won't make a sound. I'll just listen.'

'Alex is only four,' Francesca whispered to Sotiris. 'If you and the priest don't mind, then I don't. I'd hate Alex to feel he was being left out.'

Sotiris smiled back. 'He'll never feel like that with you around. For the first time in his life he feels he's got a real mother. He told me that only yesterday. We'd better move forward...'

The small choir were singing quietly now in the background as the priest began to intone the words of the service. It didn't seem to matter that Francesca couldn't understand every word. She was getting the gist of it. And with Sotiris on one side and Alex on the other she couldn't go far wrong.

Francesca noticed how relaxed the people in the chapel were. There was nothing stuffy and formal about this ceremony. Everybody was smiling, occasionally chatting quietly to their friends and relatives, even moving around from place to place. Every seat was taken and many of the guests were standing, but they didn't seem to mind. Occasionally, people would drift outside and continue to listen to the service over the external loudspeakers with the rest of the guests who'd been unable to get inside the chapel.

Francesca recognised one phrase which the choir and the priest repeated several times. *'Kyrie eleison.'* Lord have mercy. It was a haunting theme that took her back to her childhood, listening to some sacred music in a large English cathedral somewhere. Had it been Canterbury or…?

Sotiris was squeezing her hand. She turned to look at him and smiled.

'We're going to exchange rings now,' he whispered.

The priest in his gold-coloured, heavily embroidered brocade robe was leaning forward, moving their rings, first from Francesca's hand to Sotiris's hand and then the other way round so that they'd both been wearing each other's ring before they finally kept their own

The haunting Mediterranean background music was quieter now as the priest touched their foreheads before placing narrow white crowns on their heads. The crowns were joined together with ribbons, signifying that Francesca and Sotiris were now joined in holy matrimony.

Alex was tugging at her hand. She bent down, carefully, so that the crown wouldn't slip.

'I knew you were a princess,' he whispered.

She smiled. 'Like I told you, just for today.'

But she knew the feeling of being a princess would never leave her now that she had the two most wonderful people in the world as part of her own very dear family.

'Can I go out to play with my friends now you're married, Francesca?'

Francesca squeezed Alex's hand. 'Of course.'

The priest was holding a glass of wine to her lips. She took a sip. Sotiris took a sip. The priest removed their crowns. The enormity of the occasion struck home. They were married. They really were!

Friends and relatives moved easily through the little chapel now, reaching out to kiss the bride and groom. Francesca smiled, kissed, chatted quietly in English or Greek as appropriate. She felt as if she was in a dream. Her mother was there, tears brimming in her eyes as she kissed her daughter. Her father, closely following, whispered that he was so happy for her. A wonderful never-ending dream of happiness.

Light showers of rice cascaded down on them as they began to move towards the door. They were walking out into the bright sunlight now, trying not to blink as the camera flashes went off. It was a warm day but it wasn't the oppressive heat that they'd coped with during the summer months.

'I thought you were mad to suggest a late November wedding Sotiris but just look at that sky!'

Sotiris squeezed her arm. 'It's hot during the day, but it will be cooler tonight. But not too cool to have a swim in the warm sea when everybody's gone home.'

'What about Alex?' Francesca said.

Alex, having tired of the ceremony, was now playing happily at the edge of the churchyard with some of the other children

'Arwen has promised to spoil him rotten tonight when she takes him back to her house,' Sotiris said.

'He won't feel left out as he unwraps the presents I've left behind for him.'

Francesca smiled. 'That's nice. There are times when children need a bit of spoiling.'

'And times when parents need to be alone.'

'Parents,' she repeated. 'I like that.'

'You don't mind having just a one night honeymoon, do you? We can all take a holiday together in the spring or...'

'A one-night honeymoon is all I want.'

'Over here, please!' the official photographer was calling out. 'I'd like the bride and groom with relatives of the groom first.'

It took a while to round up all the Popadopoulos relatives. Sotiris had three brothers, three sisters, numerous cousins, nephews, nieces, uncles and aunts. By contrast, the Metcalfe family contingent was relatively small.

Sotiris's brothers had organised a barbecue outside the beach house. It was all so laid back, so different to some of the stiff and starchy weddings that Francesca had attended. Little by little, as the wine flowed, everybody began to let their hair down. The formal outfits were discarded. The men loosened their collars, removed their ties. The women undid the top buttons of their blouses and then the second or third, hitching up their skirts so that they could keep cool.

The numerous children ran down to the sea, paddling happily in the shallows, racing back up the beach for another morsel of barbecued chicken or some of the tiny shrimps that were one of the specialities of Ceres.

Francesca marvelled at the feast that Sotiris and his family had organised. Lamb, chicken, lobster, prawns, salads, wine, champagne...she had never seen such a spread. She tried to eat something but she was too excited, too wrapped up in the wonder of everything that was happening on this, her special day, the day she had become Sotiris's wife...

As the sun finally sank, casting a red and gold fiery glow that was reflected on the sea, everybody was in mellow mood, laughing and joking. One of Sotiris's brothers and two of his cousins had organised a small band consisting of a bouzouki, a kind of guitar, a saxophone and drums. The hauntingly evocative Greek music hung in the twilight air as people started to dance.

The men formed up in a line, pounding out their intricate steps on the hard sand at the edge of the beach while everyone clapped rhythmically in time to the music. The women joined in the dancing, bringing all the children with them. Everyone was dancing now. Francesca, leaning against the trunk of a lemon tree, watched, fascinated. She'd long since discarded her train and wedding tiara.

Sotiris came out of the beach house where he'd been organising some more wine. He walked across in front of the dancers, holding out his hands towards Francesca. She smiled and went towards him, hitching up her skirts as she saw that Sotiris wanted to dance. The music had changed. It was louder now, quicker, with a more insistent beat. Sotiris twirled her round, faster and faster. They'd never danced together like this before but she felt as if she'd been born to it. Sotiris was holding her so securely in his arms she knew she couldn't fall.

As the music ended she realised that everybody else had left the dancing area to watch them. Now they were all clapping, all coming forward to kiss the bride and groom once more.

Some of the guests were saying goodbye, others following suit as they heard the engines of the boats being started. The flotilla of boats was crossing the bay now, twinkling lights from each boat forming a decorative backdrop to their honeymoon night.

Alex had fallen asleep wrapped in a blanket under a tree but he wakened as Spiros and Arwen lifted him to take him home.

'I've got something for Francesca and Daddy,' he said, rubbing his eyes. 'My present for their honeymoon. Where did I put it, Arwen?'

'I've got it here, Alex,' she said, producing a small but bulky parcel.

'I wrapped it all by myself,' Alex said, thrusting the parcel eagerly towards Francesca.

She smiled. 'What is it, darling?'

'Go on, open it.' Alex could hardly contain his excitement.

Carefully Francesca opened the parcel and took out a glass jar.

'It's honey,' Alex said proudly. 'You can't have a honeymoon without honey. When I asked Daddy if he was going to bring some he said he'd try to remember but I think he's forgotten.'

Sotiris bent down and picked up his adorable little son. 'You're right, Alex, I did forget. Thank you ever so much.'

Francesca reached over and gave Alex a big hug and for a moment the three of them remained locked together in each other's arms.

As the boat carrying Arwen, Spiros, Natalie, Lefteris and Alex disappeared across the bay, Francesca remained still, with Sotiris's arm around her. Gently he drew her down to sit beside the dying embers of the fire which had been lit at the edge of the beach.

For a few minutes they sat together quietly, simply enjoying the peace and beauty of the bay, looking out across the water to the mysterious dark of the open sea beyond.

'Listen, I can hear the owl,' Francesca said softly.

'He's come to add his good wishes on our wedding day.'

'I remember the first time I heard the owl. The first time you brought me here. It seems so long ago now...so much has happened.'

'No regrets?'

She smiled, loving the way Sotiris's face looked so enchanting in the glow of the firelight.

'No regrets,' she whispered as she snuggled closer.

And then for the first time in that glorious day, Francesca felt a distinct chill in the air.

'You were right, Sotiris, the nights are cool now that summer's over.'

Sotiris pulled her against him, cupping her face in his hands as he looked deep into her eyes.

'We'll be very snug tonight in our little nest.'

Francesca looked up at the twinkling stars scattered over the cloudless sky. Suddenly she saw a shooting star falling, falling, disappearing into the sea. She wasn't superstitious in any way, but she made a wish just the same.

But wishes had a better chance of coming true if you did something to help them.

'Let's go to bed, Sotiris,' she whispered.

Sotiris smiled, drawing her to her feet, before scooping her up into his arms.

As her husband carried her over the threshold, Francesca felt as if she would never know such happiness again. Their wedding day had been the most wonderful day of her life.

Their wedding night, she knew, was going to be pure ecstasy...

EPILOGUE

'HAPPY anniversary, darling!' Sotiris clinked his wine glass against Francesca's.

They linked arms around the glasses and each took a sip, their heads touching.

Francesca gave a deep sigh of contented happiness. 'Doesn't seem like a year since we sat here by the sea, watching the fire in the twilight, does it? Where did the year go to, I wonder? One minute we were newly-weds…'

'And the next we were a family.' Sotiris put his head on once side as he listened. 'Was that Katerina squawking?'

Francesca laughed. 'You should know the difference between your daughter's cries and the cry of an owl by now.'

Sotiris grinned. 'Was that what it was, the owl?'

'Our owl,' Francesca said. 'He's come back to say happy anniversary. One night when Alex isn't too tired we'll keep him up so he can hear the owl.'

'He was exhausted tonight. I'm glad we only had a small party out here.'

'It was exactly right, just immediate family and a few friends. I thought Arwen looked well. When is the baby due?'

Sotiris smiled. 'In about six weeks. Arwen's over the moon at the thought of a new baby. They've been trying for another one ever since Natasha was born. Alex helped to fill in the gap but she's thrilled to be having her own baby.'

'It's going to be nice for her now that Alex is mostly with us.'

Sotiris leaned forward and kissed Francesca gently on the lips. 'Thank you for making today special.'

'I didn't have to do much. You did the barbecue. I was just here looking after our guests, swimming with the children, enjoying myself as I always do when we come to stay at the beach house.'

'You were here, and I felt…complete,' Sotiris said. 'You gave me this wonderful family and…'

'I've only given you one tiny baby.'

Sotiris smiled. 'So far.'

He tossed another log on the fire, before picking up the wine bottle from the where he'd fixed it upright in the sand.

'A little top-up?'

Francesca held out her glass. 'Why not? It's so peaceful when the children are asleep. Your mother wanted to take the children home with her for the night. She said it would be too cold for a two-month-old baby to sleep here in November. She said it wouldn't hurt Katerina to be bottle-fed until I got back tomorrow.'

'My mother hasn't experienced English weather like you and I have. This warm evening is like summer in England. Anyway, I think Katerina might be a bit of a handful for mother now she's getting older. Babies are angelic when somebody else is feeding and changing them, but if you're in sole charge it's different.'

'Your mother means well, Sotiris. She adores Katerina. It's lovely to be able to pop in for a chat during the day now that I'm not working. She's so thrilled that we called her after her own mother, your grandmother. It's a lovely name and if Katerina wants to be called Kate by her English relatives, that's OK by me.'

'I had a phone call from Paul Collins at the hospital this morning,' Sotiris said. 'He was thrilled when I phoned him soon after Katerina was born. At the time he jokingly said we might have set a record.'

Francesca smiled. 'You mean, for women who've had tubal microsurgery for infertility?'

'Exactly. He's checked among his own patients' case notes and there's only one other patient who conceived sooner than you did after Paul had performed a cornual anastomosis.'

Francesca took a sip of her wine and leaned back on the rug that covered the scrunchy sand.

'I didn't want a world record. I just wanted your baby.'

'And you don't miss working at the hospital?'

Francesca shook her head. 'I'm quite happy being a mum. It's the most satisfying job I've ever had. When they're all much older I might go back to being a doctor part time, but for the moment...'

Sotiris was smiling affectionately. 'They're all much older?' he repeated. 'We've only got two children.'

Francesca blew him a kiss across the dying embers. 'So far.'

She put her head on one side and listened. The owl had stopped hooting and the cry that she heard was definitely Katerina reminding her mum that she needed feeding.

'I'll go in and feed Katerina,' Francesca said.

'I'll come, too.'

He held out his hand and drew Francesca to her feet. She stayed for a moment leaning against him, thinking how much she loved him, how much she loved all her family. She glanced up at the sky as something caught her eye. A star was shooting across the sky, just like it had done a year ago.

She smiled. This time she wouldn't make a wish. Her wish had come true.

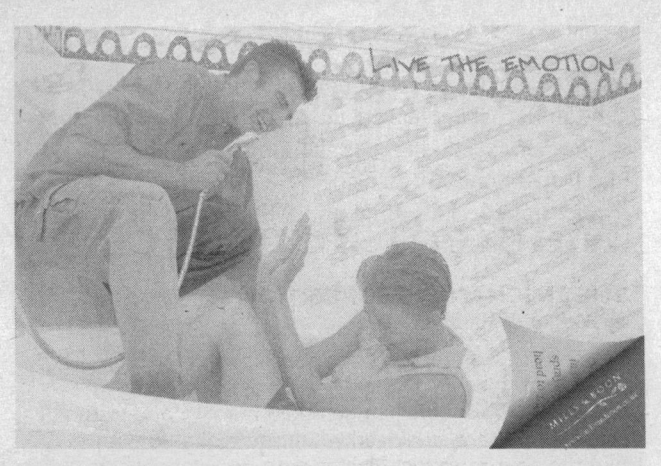

Modern Romance™
...seduction and
passion guaranteed

Tender Romance™
...love affairs that
last a lifetime

Medical Romance™
...medical drama
on the pulse

Historical Romance™
...rich, vivid and
passionate

Sensual Romance™
...sassy, sexy and
seductive

Blaze Romance™
...the temperature's
rising

27 new titles every month.

Live the emotion

MILLS & BOON®

MILLS & BOON®
Live the emotion

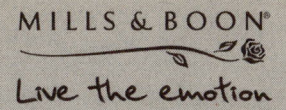

Medical Romance™

THE PREGNANCY PROPOSITION
by Meredith Webber

Nurse Amelia Peterson's relationship with A&E consultant 'Mac' McDougal had always been rocky. She was astonished when he asked her out one night ...and even more surprised when she woke up with him the next morning! Mac doesn't do relationships, but he had always wanted a child. And then Amelia realised she was pregnant...

A WHITE KNIGHT IN ER *by Jessica Matthews*

ER nurse Megan Erickson needs all the support she can get after a broken engagement and becoming mother to her brother's young children. The attention of ER physician Jonas Taylor, with his playboy reputation, is the last thing she needs. But when an accident in ER has serious implications for Megan, Jonas reveals himself as her knight in shining armour!

THE SURGEON'S CHILD *by Alison Roberts*

Consultant surgeon Matt Saunders suffered when his child's existence was kept from him, but his intimate relationship with paediatric nurse Polly Martin is the start of a passionate relationship. Soon Polly has a secret of her own – she's pregnant. Her news might push Matt away – but if she doesn't tell him, then surely he'll feel betrayed all over again?

On sale 1st August 2003

Available at most branches of WH Smith, Tesco, Martins, Borders, Eason, Sainsbury's and all good paperback bookshops.

MILLS & BOON

Live the emotion

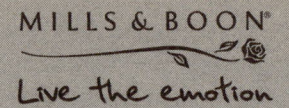

Medical Romance™

DR MARCO'S BRIDE by *Carol Wood*

Dr Marco Dallori has come to England for six months. He isn't looking for love – he's got a young son to consider, as well as his own bruised heart. Dr Kelly Anders can't help being attracted to Marco – his Latin looks are irresistible. But she knows a temporary affair is all she can hope for. Unless she can convince this Italian doctor that he needs a bride...

MEDITERRANEAN RESCUE by *Laura MacDonald*

Nurse Claire Schofield was on holiday in Rome when an earthquake threw her together with Dr Dominic Hansford. Working side by side led to one unforgettable night of pleasure, and Claire returned home with her heart full of her secret lover. But at the hospital where she now works a new locum has been appointed, and his dark good looks are *very* familiar...

THE BABY SPECIALIST by *Rebecca Lang*

When theatre nurse Leila Hardwick discovers that the new obs and gynae surgeon is Dr Rupert Daniels she tries to keep her identity secret. Her sister once tried to seduce him into having a baby. But Leila cannot escape Rupert's allure, and eventually he discovers who she is. Rupert seems as tempted by Leila as she is by him – but he avoids emotional commitment at all costs...

On sale 1st August 2003

Available at most branches of WH Smith, Tesco, Martins, Borders, Eason, Sainsbury's and all good paperback bookshops.

MILLS & BOON

STEPHANIE LAURENS

A Season for Marriage

Available from 18th July 2003

*Available at most branches of WH Smith,
Tesco, Martins, Borders, Eason, Sainsbury's
and all good paperback bookshops.*

4 FREE
books and a surprise gift!

We would like to take this opportunity to thank you for reading this Mills & Boon® book by offering you the chance to take FOUR more specially selected titles from the Medical Romance™ series absolutely FREE! We're also making this offer to introduce you to the benefits of the Reader Service™—

- ★ FREE home delivery
- ★ FREE gifts and competitions
- ★ FREE monthly Newsletter
- ★ Exclusive Reader Service discount
- ★ Books available before they're in the shops

Accepting these FREE books and gift places you under no obligation to buy, you may cancel at any time, even after receiving your free shipment. Simply complete your details below and return the entire page to the address below. *You don't even need a stamp!*

YES! Please send me 4 free Medical Romance books and a surprise gift. I understand that unless you hear from me, I will receive 6 superb new titles every month for just £2.60 each, postage and packing free. I am under no obligation to purchase any books and may cancel my subscription at any time. The free books and gift will be mine to keep in any case.

M3ZEE

Ms/Mrs/Miss/Mr ....Initials..
BLOCK CAPITALS PLEASE

Surname ....

Address ....

....

....Postcode.................................

Send this whole page to:
UK: FREEPOST CN81, Croydon, CR9 3WZ
EIRE: PO Box 4546, Kilcock, County Kildare (stamp required)

Offer valid in UK and Eire only and not available to current Reader Service subscribers to this series. We reserve the right to refuse an application and applicants must be aged 18 years or over. Only one application per household. Terms and prices subject to change without notice. Offer expires 31st October 2003. As a result of this application, you may receive offers from Harlequin Mills & Boon and other carefully selected companies. If you would prefer not to share in this opportunity please write to The Data Manager at the address above.

Mills & Boon® is a registered trademark owned by Harlequin Mills & Boon Limited.
Medical Romance™ is being used as a trademark.